INTRODUCTION

….truth is always strange;
Stranger than fiction: if it could be told,
How much would novels gain by the exchange!
How differently the world would men behold!
from *Don Juan,* by Lord Byron

I can't claim that Nethergate Writers had these words in mind when they took up the challenge offered by Angus and Dundee Roots Festival 2008 to produce a collection of work themed around their ancestors. What I do know is that in researching their material they uncovered some fascinating local history and were introduced to numerous unforgettable characters from the area's past.

Angus is sometimes described as Scotland's birthplace so it's fitting that the collection opens with a story set in the first century AD. *The Knowing* by Cathy Whitfield is a haunting account of a young boy's rite of passage. We are certainly struck by the strangeness of his world yet, by the magic of fiction and the skill of the writer, we can still identify with his hopes and fears almost two thousand years on.

In *The Homecoming* by Christine Mercier, past and present are linked in a surprising way as we move to Dundee in 1620, a time when there was mass emigration from Scotland to Poland. Many Dundonians established themselves as traders, like the character in the story, while many became pre-eminent in Polish society while maintaining their links back home.

From Dundee we move to Cortachy in the Angus Glens and to the church which stood next to Cortachy Castle, the seat of the Ogilvies of Airlie since 1625, and still home to Lord Airlie. In *Ann Sneeshin's Snuffbox* Flora Davidson conjures up not just a set of characters at a Kirk Session meeting in 1763 but the entire world of the Glen at that time, all with great economy and wit.

From the world of ordinary folk we move back to Dundee and an encounter with a true Dundee hero. Bob Drysdale retells an incident from the run-up to the 1797 Battle of Camperdown in his extract from a fictional biography of the great man, entitled *Admiral Duncan and the Phantom Fleet.*

The character in Ed Thompson's *The Sporting Life* is not so much hero as anti-hero. Stroll with him through the streets of Dundee and you will be able to smell the smells, hear the sounds, and see the sights of the city in 1820 as you enjoy a rollicking and robust tale. Move forward just eleven years to 1831 and the picture of the city widens as we are introduced to the much more respectable face of a thriving and intellectually stimulating Dundee in Ann Prescott's beautifully observed *Gleaners of Nature.*

Byron's view that truth is stranger than fiction might just be challenged in the next story, *Dead Ed,* by Gill Blackmore. Switching between East Haven in 1848 and the present, this is a compelling tale that reminds us of the ever present threat of death and disease in the lives of our ancestors. Death occurred not just as the result of disease, however. In her story, *Small Sacrifices,* Beth Blackmore reveals the real price of jute in

ROOTS

First published in Great Britain in 2008 by Nethergate Writers,
Department of Continuing Education,
University of Dundee,
Nethergate,
Dundee, DD1 4HN
Second impression June 2008

Edited by Esther Read
Chosen by Dr. James Stewart

Cover design by Rikki O'Neill. Website: www.RIKOART.co.uk

Nethergate Writers gratefully acknowledge the financial assistance
of Sir James Cayzer and Dundee University's Extra-Mural
Students' Association towards the publication of this volume

ISBN 978-0-9555831-1-7

British Library Cataloguing in Publication Data
A catalogue record for this book is available from the British Library

CONTENTS

ACKNOWLEDGEMENTS

The Nethergate Writers who are collectively the authors of *Roots* are members of Dundee University's Continuing Education class, 'Continuing as a Writer.' We acknowledge with pleasure our many debts of gratitude – not least to the Department of Continuing Education for running the class and for supporting us throughout.

The Extra-Mural Students' Association provided generous financial support towards the publication of *Roots,* as did Sir James Cayzer of Newtyle, whose contribution to the arts is never sufficiently acknowledged. Henny King, Director of Angus and Dundee Roots Festival, was an invaluable source of advice and suggestions. Rikki O'Neill designed the cover of *Roots,* patiently making one change after another to accommodate our wishes as they developed.

We are greatly indebted to Dr Jim Stewart, who teaches Creative Writing in the University's English Department. He made the final selection of scripts for publication, and gave each of us a very useful critique.

Above all it is Esther Read that we have to thank for the success of the project. As Class Tutor she initiated the *Roots* project at the beginning of the session, and during the next two terms worked ceaselessly to help us respond to it. She then changed hats and as editor saw *Roots* through the intricacies of proofreading, layout, illustration and printing.

Edward H. Thompson
Chair, Nethergate Writers, 2008

her moving and dramatic story of one Dundee mill girl in the mid-1800s.

Yet town girls weren't the only ones to be suffering at this time. The balance of power between the farmer and his workers is revealed in Jean Langland's story, *Mrs Dargie's Revenge*, where a misunderstanding leads to a tragic outcome. But change was afoot in the countryside as elsewhere, as the character in David Carson's *The Coffin Road* (set in 1880) discovers when he returns to the Glen, after a five year absence, to attend his brother's funeral .

As David's character travels in an unexpected direction, we move back to Dundee and another example of the city's industrial heritage – the whaling and shipping trades. Lesley Holmes's *The Ballad O' The Chieftain* retells, in traditional ballad form, one of the city's most famous whaling misadventures, that of 'The Chieftain' in 1884. Roddie McKenzie in *The Old Man and the C* (the 'C' also referring to the Chieftain) reprises the story from the viewpoint of one of the survivors - but with a wonderful comic twist. Meantime Amanda Barclay in *Blackheart* examines the civilian side of dock life in her finely understated story set in the offices of the Gem Line Steam Shipping Company in the 1890s.

Many of the themes of these stories of Dundee in the 1890s are brought together in *Two For The Price of One* by Faye Stevenson which ingeniously interweaves three timeframes, the 1900s, 1940s and the present, to tell the story of Grey Lodge Settlement and its impact on Dundee citizens past and present.

For a complete change of mood we now switch to

Carnoustie in 1929, around the time when hickory clubs were being dropped from golf championships in favour of the new steel-shafted variety. In his delightful story, *Mallet,* John Mooney charts the results of this golfing revolution.

Change, of whatever sort, is often the catalyst for a story so it's perhaps no surprise that no fewer than four of the pieces record the upheaval in the lives of those who lived through the Second World War. In *Ba, Ba, Da, Da* by Jane O'Neill, we have a vivid reminder of life in Dundee at that time as seen through the eyes of a young child whose family life is disintegrating almost as rapidly as the world around her. In Nan Rice's *The Funeral* we switch between the 1940s and the present to unravel the story of how one young girl chose to redress what she saw as the injustices of her life. The truth, when it's uncovered, proves to be a shock for her son while there's another shock for the character in Gaye Manwaring's *Between The Lines* as she discovers the truth behind her mother's time at the Air Base in Montrose.

However, the War didn't just leave bombed buildings and wrecked lives in its wake. It radically altered the social order of things – as the lady's maid in *Change of Address* by Catherine Young discovers. Set in Broughty Ferry and Dundee in 1946, this story vividly evokes the atmosphere of the time.

Last, but by no means least, for a unique overview of Dundee, try *Twa Gulls and Three Js* by David Francis. If this doesn't have you laughing out loud, I'll be surprised.

Esther Read, 2008

THE KNOWING

Cathy Whitfield

To begin with there is only the wind and the rock and the sound the two make together. A grey sound in a grey place, a cold place in the wreathed grip of fog, stone unwarmed by sun, wan in the half-light of a sun gone pallid with moisture.

There is moisture in the air but none on the ground. Not up here on the summit of the sacred mountain. There is neither pool nor stream. Only the sound, half-way down the mountain, of water running. From further away, below in the valley, comes the howl of a lone wolf. Nearer, invisible in the clinging shifting cloud, a raven quarks as it tumbles on the wind. Then silence again. Just wind and rock and the sound the two make together. And from half-way down the mountain the sound of water running, agonisingly far away.

Agonisingly far away. That is a man's thought, thinks the boy. Only a man can take a sound and give it a shape it lacked before. He listens quite deliberately to the sound of water and lets his thirst shape the sound to longing. He has not eaten since the fall of night on the previous day and for a time hunger had stalked him but it no longer does so. He has not drunk either for the whole of the night's walk to the base of the mountain nor for the day's climb to its summit although he had crossed stream after stream and each time the not drinking had been harder. His thirst is sharper now but in time that too will go. And then will come the Knowing.

Sounds taking shape is part of it, he thinks, sounds being given shape. He waits for shape to shiver back into sound, for rock to blur and give voice - the grind of stone on stone - and wonders if light will quiver into music. He hears his own heart as the beat of a skin drum, the breath whistling in his throat like the song of a bone flute. But the light remains the same, as flat and pallid as dead flesh.

He had killed his first man only two days before. A man of the Taexali tribe, a spear thrust in the chest. A quick, clean kill. The priests marked his face with the blood and even now the marks tighten his skin; the spirit marks of the oldest ones who pocked the sun-stones with the same patterns. He had sat all that night beside the body, as was the custom, waiting for the sun to take the man's spirit. He had seen it in the first rays of morning, a faint breath of spirit thinning into the wind. The man was not much older than himself, but marked as a man with the bull sign of the Taexali, his flesh, by daylight, as flat and pallid as sun shining through thin cloud.

The priests sent him to the mountain after that, that he might find the Knowing and become a man. But first, they told him, he must cast loose the bindings of his boyhood flesh and swear neither to eat nor drink until he returns. It is a setting free, he understands, an emptying of the spirit so that the Knowing can take its place. They had warned him he would see things that were not truly there, that he would see things that were and not believe them. Only the Knowing will let him distinguish one from the other, and the Knowing is the gift of the God to man. When he returns from the mountain they will mark him as a man of the Venicones, the stag-tribe.

The boy walks on, the rocks tilting beneath his aching feet. He is colder now, naked to the wind, for all protection was taken from him; his leather kilt, his sheepskin vest, his twin spears and his charm of protection – the eagle feather tied with a thread of three colours. Up here on the God's mountain there is no protection but the oath he has sworn; the three-fold oath that only a man may swear - or a boy sent to the mountain to find the Knowing.

May the sky fall on me, the earth gape and swallow me, the sea burst out and overwhelm me.

Up here, in the clouds, he feels the weight of the sky.

He's dizzy now, the mist swirling behind his eyes. He sees a scatter of strangely shaped rocks and it is some time before he recognises them as bones bleached by the sun and scattered by ravens. Further on, beneath an overhang, lies a skull, still with shreds of dried skin and hair adhering to it, the blank sockets staring into the blind sun. There are those who seek the Knowing and do not return. He remembers such a one who had killed his man earlier that year in a spring raid on the Vacomagi, a boy who failed to return from the mountain.

He finds his stone close by the scattered body; a pale

stone the size of his fist, marked with a darker streak. Recognising the stone is the beginning, and thereafter omens start to cluster. The body of the boy who failed to return falls behind in the mist but soon he finds the gold - a disk the size of his thumbnail, incised with the salmon mark - a good omen. Further on lies another and further still a group of discs that once were the necklace of a chieftain. The priests bring the bodies of the great ones to lie on the summit of the God's mountain, as gifts for the ravens.

Perhaps his Knowing will take the form of a raven for the God has many forms and this is one of them. The God has many names and only the priests can speak them all, but the boy knows a few; Arddhu, the dark one; Kernhe, the horned one; Bran the raven. He has heard the raven cry, the wolf howl, but no stag bark. It would be good if the God was to take shape as the stag, his tribe's totem. But perhaps it will be the winter hare, who is sacred to the moon, or the bull who bears the sun between his horns. Even the serpent - although that would mark him as a priest and not a warrior.

It is darker now, the sun dropping into deeper cloud, the day ending. The raid had been unseasonably late in the year, long past the Lughnasaidh horse-fair, and in barely a moon's passing it will be Samhain, Feast of the Dead. He hopes his will not be one of the spirits made welcome at this year's feast. This unbidden thought is not a good one, a careless thought that lets fear take shape. Cold is forgotten, thirst a thing of the past, hunger almost unimagined. All he has now, naked on the God's mountain, is fear.

His feet falter and the dead press close - the boy with his raven-empty eyes, the gold-girt chieftain, the warriors who died in battle, the priests who see all things. The dead judge him, their spirits measuring his lack and the weight of their judgement presses on him like the sky. He wishes the earth would gape and swallow his shame, the sea rise up and overwhelm his fear. He falls to his knees and then his hands. He crawls the rest of the way, his belly to the ground, approaching the God as a serpent among the rocks. But still he holds the stone and the gold disc.

The way steepens through great slabs of stone split and shattered by the winter. They cut his hands and knees until his skin is slicked with blood, but he keeps going, onward and upward, until there is nowhere else to go. Ahead of him is the cairn of warriors; a mound of stones perched on the highest place. Beside it lies a pile of gold. He stares at the gold, his vision swimming, and it blinds him. The day, that had been darkening, now splits open, carved by a ray of sun, as the clouds part.

The boy gets to his knees, places his own stone on the cairn, his gold disc joining others in the coruscating glimmer of unimagined wealth. He gets to his feet. Fear is gone, leaving behind a spirit wiped clean and ready for revelation. He walks past the cairn, to the great prow of the hill. Vertigo takes him and he is dizzy with distance. Far below he sees, as if his eyes are those of an eagle, circling in the sky, the land of Circinn – his land. It lies spread out beneath him, layer upon layer, diminishing into the distance until it meets the hard flat glitter of the sea. Behind him on the summit of the sacred mountain will stand the God of his people, the one who holds up the sky with one hand, the Knowing in his other.

He turns slowly. A raven tumbles on the wind, crying as it does so, angling across the crest of the ridge. To one side a hare dips between rocks. Above him an eagle tilts and soars. But none of them is the God. He feels eyes on him, hears the wind breathe slow, a growl of gravel deep in its throat. He hears the slow, slow, thud of a heart beating out the seasons. His own heart beats light and fast, and his breath catches as he makes the final turn and sees ...

He sees nothing.

Only the cairn. Only the gold. Only the long ridge-back of grey stone pallid with remembered moisture. A shred of fog flees like a spirit on the wind. Perhaps it is his own.

But then he sees another thing, a little thing he had not noticed before - a plane of rock, flat beneath the sky, hollowed by wind and water to a smooth bowl. Within it, glinting and ruffling, lies a little pool of water.

Thirst spears him and floods the empty place inside him. There is nothing now but thirst. He crouches beside the pool on bloodied knees and stares into the basin of rainwater that holds nothing more than a handful of gravel. He has sworn the three-fold oath that he will not drink, and yet he knows that if he does not he will die here on the mountain. If he denies himself the water he will crouch beneath a rock, as had the dead-eyed boy, and in the cold of the night he will die.

This then is the Knowing, this then the choice. He leans
forward and sees a reflection – but it is not the reflection of
a boy who has come to find the Knowing. He smiles when
he recognises it, and his bloodied hands break the surface to
shatter the image of the smiling face. He slakes his thirst
down to the very bottom of the pool, and it tastes better
than anything he has ever tasted.

The sky sails steadily above him. The earth bulks beneath
him and fails to open. The sea remains a rumour in the
distance.

He gets to his feet, reclaims the gold disc and sets off
back along the ridge. Later, he will bind the disc to the first
of his warrior braids, beside his eagle's feather. The priests
will mark him as a man of the tribe, prick out the symbols
with their fine bone needles and the blue stain. There will be
the salmon of knowledge for the disc, the stag for his tribe,
and the caste marks of crescent and spear. For his warrior
sept they will mark him with the creature whose form the
God took in his Knowing. He will tell them it was a raven.
But he knows now that the God takes no form, for the God
who bears all names is all forms, even that of the creature
who stared at him from the surface of a pool of water.
Himself. And yet not himself.

This is the Knowing, worthy of the mountain, worthy
of a man of the Venicones. That is a man's thought, thinks
the man as he makes his way down the track, singing as he
goes. That is a good thought.

THE HOMECOMING

Christine Mercier

Dundee sparkles under the morning sun as Captain Fairweather steers the *Grace* past the breakwater and into harbour to moor her alongside the stone pier.

Jamie Cramer has been up on deck since before dawn, watching the green coast materialise out of the darkness. It is five years since he last saw his home and now, after ten long days at sea, his feet are itching to get back on land.

Grace bumps and judders as her ropes are thrown ashore and secured. Her tall masts groan as the sailors pull down and fold the sails. The men attack their work with added vigour, now that they can hear the harbour whores calling from the dockside.

Since her first sighting in the Tay the merchants have been gathering on the quayside, eager to unload their cargoes and to collect news from their Baltic representatives. The shoremaster stands with his tallysheet, ready to calculate taxes and dues.

"Haud firm."

"Steady as she goes."

"More to starboard."

Jamie holds tightly onto his pack as the gangplank is let

down and the travellers jostle towards the side of the boat. *Grace* dips a little and knocks against the quayside.

"Haud back, ye buggers," shouts the crewman, pressing them back. "Ye'll aa get ashore in guid time - if ye dinna capsize her first."

Jamie feels a strong hand on his shoulder.

"You bastar', Jamie! You want go 'way without say goodbye?"

"Mister Piotr!" Jamie turns to see a swarthy face embellished with a fine moustache close to his own. "I was meaning to wait for you down at the harbour, sir."

"Hrrr. Harbour too late. Harbour - I must see cargo unload - I must meet Mister Wedderburn - I have many business."

Piotr manhandles him towards the abandoned far side of the deck. He pulls Jamie's pack from him, places it roughly on the boards and pushes him down onto it, then seats himself astride a pile of coiled rope to face him. "Now," he growls, "We talk."

"Mister Piotr ..."

"No ... no... you listen me. What is problem? We discuss."

"There are things I have to do, Mister Piotr. I've nae been hame for five years... I don't know if I will want to go back to Danzig..."

"You young bastar', you all same!" Piotr reaches inside the large woollen coat which has not left his back throughout the voyage and draws out a bottle. He takes a swig and hands it to Jamie. "Drink," he orders.

Jamie knows it is useless to protest. He has long since learnt how to let the fiery spirit slip down without catching his throat, but although it no longer makes him splutter, he feels its kick somewhere at the back of his head.

He hands back the bottle blindly. Piotr laughs and punches his chest. "You good bastar', Jamie. You go - settle business in Dundee, then you come find Piotr before this boat go back. I already speak Mr. Wedderburn's brother before we leave. He like you, he trust you like son. We make good work for you. Five more years in Danzig, you learn drink like real Polak!"

With the rocking gait of a man newly ashore Jamie walks through the harbourside throng and crosses to the fishmarket. There is a stink that he never noticed in the old days, when he played with fish heads under the trestles while his mother gutted and sold herring.

He does not know whether anyone will recognise him, now that he is no longer a boy of fourteen, but grown to full manhood and clothed in foreign jerkin and breeks. But there is to be no by-passing.

"Hoy," cries Elspet Barry, her voice deep and salted as any sailor's. "Is that nae you Jamie Cramer, slitherin' past yer ain folk like a pious stranger?"

She throws down her knife and her half-gutted fish and waddles towards him on her swollen purple legs and stretches up to fold him in her fishy arms as if he were one of her own bairns. And now the other fishwomen surround him, wiping down their bloody hands on their skirts while they exclaim how tall he has grown, how fine he looks and how proud poor Isobel would be if she could see him now.

And they ply him with questions. Where he has been these past times? How has he fared in those strange lands? How long will he stay in Dundee? So many questions that he stutters and laughs as he answers. He blushes as they poke his intimates and exchange ribaldries about travels into foreign parts...

He recognises Agnes Kyd and Janet Melville - and then his own aunt Effie who is shouting and crying all at the same time, and pulling at his sleeve to take him to her house and tell the bairns that Jamie is come back. And she is shouting to all that will listen that this is a great day, that there has not been such a day since the King himself came to Dundee a few years back - him that was James VI but is now gone to be rightful king of England.

And Jamie promises that he will come to her house, for he has no home of his own to sleep in, since his mother is dead and his father too, for all he cares. But first, he tells her, he has something he must attend to, something that cannot wait. And he tears himself away from the women and breaks into a run past St. Clement's Manse and along Skirling's Wynd, past the luckenbooths in the mercat into the narrow wynds beyond. And now everything is familiar to him and he is light-hearted in the knowledge that he is in Dundee, he is home.

The streets wind up away from the river, keeping out the

worst of the winds from the houses on either side. He knows the door he is seeking, though the thought crosses his mind that perhaps she has flitted? But if she has gone he will ask after her; someone will know where he can find her.

And here is the door - somehow smaller and more rotted than he remembers. This is where she lived all the time that he knew her, where once she cared for her sickly mother. He hesitates a moment then raps nervously. There is silence. He knocks again and tries to push the door. There is a scratching sound as the latch lifts.

The door opens slowly. A bairn - a skeletal waif, three maybe four years old - stands and stares.

He hears a voice from inside, a crude guttural voice he does not know. "Come awa here, Meg. How oft hae eh telt ye no tae gang tae the door?" But the girl - he knows now that it is a girl - rubs the green snot from her nose with the back of her hand and continues to stare.

There is a clatter inside the room, a rasping cough and a few steamy words before a woman appears in the doorway. A second child is hanging off her hip and a third is pushing out her belly. She snatches the girl's shoulder, without looking up.

"Eh've nae rent tae gie ye - eh telt ye yisterday," she spits. "Can ye no leave us alane?"

"Maggie?" The question is real for he recognises nothing in this carlin.

She lifts her face and frees the child to sweep back the lank hair from her eyes and stare at him brazenly.

"Maggie! It is you?"

She turns quickly and pushes the two children roughly before her into the house. "Go awa," she hisses over her shoulder. "Eh dinnae ken ye."

But he forces his way and follows her in. "Maggie, Maggie! I said I would come back. Do ye no remember?"

They are in the room now. It is colder than outside. As his eyes accustom to the grim light seeping in from the open door - there is no window - he realises that in all his travels he has not seen such destitution. The stone walls are running with moisture and fungus grows in the corner where an uncovered bucket stands half full of orange liquid and excrement. The smell catching his nostrils makes his stomach heave and he turns away quickly. Even in the depths of the *Grace* there was nothing like this.

Maggie sits down on the bed and looks up at him sullenly. The bairns are clinging to her knees, watching intently. "Well?" she mumbles. "Whit hae ye come fer?"

He does not know what to answer. So many times in those five years he has thought of her and of his promise to her, but his vision of her sweet untouched body was so different to this, that now he really does not know what to answer.

"Maggie, I ... I..."

She laughs - a cold sardonic laugh that shows up the lines on her face and reveals that she is lacking several teeth. "Ye were ne'er a wan wi' words, Jamie Cramer." She pushes away wee Meg who is trying to climb onto her lap with a whimpering, "I'm cold, ma."

And Jamie remembers his gift, so carefully chosen. He takes the green shawl from his sack. Its bright red flowers look garish in these grey surroundings. The fringe tickles his fingers as he shakes it open to show her.

Maggie looks down at the earthen floor. "I want naethin fae ye," she murmurs. "Just go awa' and lea' us alane."

But the little girl has come shyly to his side. Her eyes are wide and her sore-covered mouth is open. She stretches out a hand and dares to touch. "Eh!"

Jamie drops to his knees beside her. "It's fur yer ma. Dae ye like it?" The child stands still and says nothing. He tries not to recoil from the smell of her thin body as he wraps the shawl around her. She hugs it and spins towards her mother, smiling at last. "Eh … ma …"

Maggie snatches the shawl so fiercely that the child spins and falls to the ground. She throws it at Jamie in fury. "Git oot!" she cries. "Git oot!"

He has no choice but to go, yet his mind is confused as he stumbles from the dark cold room into the dark street, leaving the shawl in the dirt where it fell. The morning's elation has passed.

What has become of the Maggie he knew, the girl with whom he once shared his dreams? With whom he watched from Castle Hill the tall ships sailing into harbour with their cargoes of wines from Burgundy, and olive oil from Spain, and herring from the Isles, and timber from Norroway, and grain from faraway Danzig?

And what has become of the boy Jamie? Does he still exist, the lad who hungered to know what lay beyond the Argyle Gate and the Well Gate, beyond the hills that surround Dundee?

He has kept his promise. He has returned with his little bag of merks and ducats, crowns and franks, which he keeps inside his shirt, next to his skin. Why will she not talk to him, why can she not tell him how this has all come about?

As he blindly follows the wynd down into the Murraygate he hears running from the Shambles and his name being called: "Whaur are ye, Jamie Cramer?"

And Effie's boys, Davy and Rabbie, burst round the corner laughing and shouting.

"Eh Jamie - ye look like a birkie in them breeks!"

"Ma telt us ye wis hame - she's sent us tae bring ye back."

And as they hug and thump each other, he notices how his cousins too have changed - they are men now, like himself, not the boys that he left behind.

"We dinna need to gang hame yet," insists Rabbie. "We cannae pass Jak's and nae celebrate Jamie's hamecomin."

It is quiet in the dark fuggy bar, for it is scarcely past noon and neither the sailors nor the shoremen have finished their work. Rabbie sets up beakers of ale and they drink and talk, and talk and drink, and decide to have one more jar before they take him home to Effie.

And then the door scrapes open. The air falls very still. Davy is staring over Jamie's shoulder. Rabbie sets down his ale.

Jamie turns on his stool and sees a large man crossing the

23

room, his face bristling with stubble and with anger. In a few strides he is beside them and sticking his left fist under Jamie's chin, lifting him to his feet.

"Ye," he spits. "The foreign bastar' wha's been interferin wi ma wife." In his right hand he holds the shawl, its fringe dripping with orange liquid, its colours no longer so bright.

Jamie tries to shake his head free, but the grip only tightens. Davy jumps to his feet as the shawl is wiped over Jamie's face.

"Calm yersel, Andrew," he says softly. "He didnae ken ..."

"Haud yer wheesht!"

Davy drops back, his face pallid. Other drinkers behind him are sliding away into the shadows. Big Jock has moved out from behind the bar.

"Nane o' tha' in here," he growls. "Ootside, the baith o' ye."

Jamie looks furtively around the room. There is a small door at the back. If he can get to it, it will take him out onto Castle Hill.

But his thought is too late. Big Jock is behind, pushing him towards the door, while Andrew pulls in the same direction. Everyone else has frozen. Andrew's arms and skull are too thick to brook any protest.

Out in Skirling's Wynd, Jamie is thrown against the wall. He feels a crushing kick between his thighs which bends his body in two, and then a blow cracks across his nose. Then Andrew's knee is in his stomach and his fists are battering his head, again and again and again. He hears a roaring in his brain, like the howl of the wind on the night the *Grace* sailed out of the Baltic into the North Sea. He feels a sickness in his gut, a spinning in his head, a blinding pressure at the back of his eyes.

He slumps to the ground, but still Andrew does not stop. He kicks in fury at his face, at his stomach, at his throat. He stamps on Jamie's legs and kicks again and again. Then, as Jamie passes into blackness, he turns and runs.

"Jemmy! Jemmy! Jemmy!"

He tries to raise his head, but pain prevents him. He succeeds in half-opening his eyelids and sees a face above his own, a black moustache like the outline of a ship on the sea.

"You young bastar', you make me fright, I think you dead!"

Piotr is kneeling beside him. He has covered Jamie with his greatcoat. He reaches inside his jerkin and pulls out a bottle. "You open mouth," he orders.

Jamie has no strength to protest. He feels the liquid run over his face and pour between his lips, feels the shock as it hits the gap where teeth are missing. There is a sharp taste on his swollen tongue before the cocktail of blood and spirit hits the back of his throat.

Piotr nods approvingly. "You live," he says.

Davy too is kneeling beside him, crying like a boy. "Jamie - I'm sorry, I couldna help ye ... abody kens that Andrew's a madman ... he wud hae kilt ye, if he hadna came." He flicks his thumb towards Piotr.

Jamie tries to lift his head again, but he feels his stomach heave painfully and a rush of sour vomit spills out of his mouth, ale and blood and vodka mixed with all his hopes and his dreams, and all the aspiration and joy of his homecoming.

He leans back against the wall, choking, and lets the spinning universe of blackness and stars settle in his head. Every part of his body is throbbing; he wants to sleep.

"Ma'll kill us," he hears Rabbie whisper.

"You lisen me," says Piotr, looking ruefully at his coat. "Now you sick, young bastar', you head is hurt, you think you want die. But maybe no bones is broken. Two days - maybe three - you feel better. I have speak Mister Wedderburn - you come back with me to Danzig. I think you have finish business in Dundee."

ANN SNEESHIN'S SNUFFBOX

Flora Davidson

The Kirk Officer had banked up the peat fire in the Cortachy Session Room when the Clerk arrived. "Aye Mr Doig, you'll be glad o a fire the day. This rain will turn to snaw afore ye're feenished."

"I doubt we'll not get muckle of a turnout fae Clova," Mr Doig said conversationally, rubbing cold hands. "The Esk is lipping ower already."

"Ye'll ken Sneeshin's deid, Mr Doig?"

"Mphm?"

Surprisingly, the farmers from Clova nearly all arrived, except Lindsay in Bonhard. "The Kirkton brig has birled doon the water again. He'll no win ower to the road." Ogilvy in Buss was unafraid of the long ride home through floods, but his cousin was opting to stay with the Ogilvys at Rottal. His squat figure in great cowhide boots obscured the fire from the others.

"You'll never get ower the ford to Rottal, neither will Mitchell," Ogilvy in Tarrybuckle observed with gloomy relish as Mitchell unwound his sodden plaid and shouldered the others aside to get a share of the fire.

His place was soon usurped by Brocklaws, declaring, "Kinrive burn is fairly roarin doon."

The five burly Elders, important with office, steamed before the fire while five round bonnets dripped on the coat pegs and a leather-covered flask of usquebae circulated without comment.

The Minister, the Treasurer, the Ruling Elder and the local merchant all entered together and four sopping hats joined the country bonnets. Mr Doig rose and bowed to the Minister, nodded to his brother-in-law and glunched at the Menmuir man that had wormed his way in and was now Treasurer. On the merchant's heels Braeside burst in, streaming water, last as usual and him closest to the kirk.

Mr Doig wrote in his minute-book: '*December 4th, 1763. Sederunt Mr Ogilvy the Minister, Jno Blair, And & Thos Ogilvys, R Duncan, R Mitchell, And & Geo Edwards, Jas Dury, Jas Guthrie. The Meeting opened with Prayer.*'

"So Sneeshin's deid," the Treasurer observed. "That's anither pauper funeral we've to pey for. On the tap o shoon to the orphan."

At his elbow the Session Clerk flipped back a page of the Kirk Session Minutes and read out, "Shoes to the orphan £1.10/- Scots, inde half-a-crown Sterling. Dr Ogilvy of Forfar -"

Mr Ogilvy, the Minister, coughed warningly. "Not the now, Mr. Doig - Sneeshin?" His mind running on snuff, his hand moved unconsciously to his pocket and halted, chastened.

"Aye sir, Ann Sneeshin the gangin-aboot body, fund deid

in the shippen at Fichel."

A.S., vagrant, wrote the Session Clerk, *found dead in Fichel's shed.* There was a general smile and head-shaking at the news. "Guid old Annie. We'll miss her."

"She canna hae just an ordinar pauper funeral."

"She will have left something," said the Treasurer. "Did we no allow her a sum for clothing the other day, month, or whatever? That can be rouped."

"I doot no," cackled Tarrybuckle. "It was a year or mair back and Ann's no famous for washing."

His neighbour chimed in, "They say her sarks is movin wi lice. The weemen that streekit her has cast them on the midden."

"Tut-tut. Surely the shirts could have been cleaned." The Minister frowned. Lack of snuff was affecting his nerves.

"What aboot the skirt-length we gied her in Agust? Her skirt should bring in enough to gie the puir sowl breid and ale tae her funeral."

"Aye, Rab, if onybody will bid for a skirt wi lice inclusive."

The Clerk turned back to read, '*August 28th, 1762, to 3 ells of Gray & making thereof to Ann Sneeshing £3.*'

"Was that really her name?" queried the Minister, drumming tensely on the table.

"Ane o her names," answered Brocklaws. "Whiles she's Ann Lindsay but maistly Ann Ogilvy. Wi her wey o't, her faither was a merchant and her mither a fermer's dochter."

The Clerk silently practised his English: *with her way of it a farmer's daughter.*

"She was a foundlin laid at my faither's door," said the Ruling Elder flatly. "It depends on whaur she's begging. At Gella and Wheen and the Eggies she said her faither was an Ogilvy, but aroond Fichel he was a Lindsay. Whatever the fermer there is himsel."

The Ogilvys looked defensive. The Clerk mouthed, *Whatever the farmer is himself.* He was not the Schoolmaster for nothing.

"She was aye guid entertainment, though. When her and Cairnie met at onybody's hoose they metaphorically clawed ilk other's een oot. He couldna stand her, nor she him."

Clawed each other's een, no, eyes, out.

"He'd maybe heard that tale o hers aboot him getting himsel hurled aboot in a barrow, letting on to be cripple. He was left at Clachnabrain's door to beg, she said, but Clachnabrain never cam oot and never cam oot till Cairney was that disgusted he hopped oot o the barrow and hurled it awa himsel." Tarrybuckle's laugh got mixed up with a rheumy cough that gave the laugh a run for its money.

Mr Doig lost the thread of the discourse wracking his brain for the English. He found *'wheeled it away himself'* and returned to taking notes.

"I'll tell you better than that," the Minister said, forgetting his fret for a moment. "There was one time she craved alms at me and I said, Honest woman, I said, I have nothing less than a sixpence in my pocket. – I can gie you change, says she, and produces fivepence from hers. I was that surprised I handed over my sixpence. Well! She bit it to see if it was genuine, and adjured me to test her fivepence likewise. But if she was an Ogilvy, or even a Lindsay, how do you call her Ann Sneeshin?"

"Oh sir, did she never crave sneeshin fae you? She was aye haudin oot her snuffbox to be filled. A demon for the sneeshin, oor Ann."

The Minister sighed.

"So whaur's it noo? It should be rouped wi the rest o her belongings. Wha's got it noo?" The Treasurer looked round accusingly.

There was a long indignant silence. At last the Minister put it to the vote how much might be allotted to the pauper funeral. The Ogilvys voted for a supplement to the usual sum. Though his wife was a Lindsay, Mitchell abstained. Lindsay of Bonhard was, of course, absent. The uninvolved shilly-shallied.

Eleven pounds one shilling was spent on Ann's funeral for there was a big turnout. The next week there was another pauper funeral to be ordered – Cairney's. He being less popular and neither an Ogilvy nor a Lindsay, there was no question of supplement – until the Kirk Officer knocked at the Session Room door to deliver a message from the women who had washed the corpse.

They had found the only saleable item among the beggar's rags, a brass snuffbox. The elders sat up. They looked at the battered object before them.

The Minister opened it. He sniffed at the contents. "Black rappee," he murmured ecstatically as with difficulty he refrained from helping himself. "The best. Eminently roupable. Maybe we can extend the usual sum for a pauper."

Reluctantly he relinquished the snuffbox to the Treasurer.

"That's Annie's box," said both Ogilvys. "Aye is't," chimed in Mitchell.

"And we'll no let that auld Cairney profit from theft."

So the Clerk wrote in his minute-book, '*To Cairney's funeral £6 Scots. Snuffbox, property of the deceased Ann Lindsay or Ogilvy, commonly known as Ann Sneeshin, instantly rouped for 1/8 Sterling, which sum was placed in the Poorbox.*'

"And now, if there is no other business," said the Minister, radiant, "Let us close the Meeting with Prayer."

Dundee   1797

ADMIRAL DUNCAN AND THE PHANTOM FLEET
An extract from the biography of the late
Admiral Sir James Campbell of Pitlochry.

Bob Drysdale

In the spring of 1797 I was flag lieutenant to Admiral Adam
Duncan, a fellow Scot, from Dundee, aboard his flag ship
the 74 gun *Venerable* lying off Yarmouth.

It was a difficult time for the service. The war with
Revolutionary France was not going well and despite the
victory at Cape St Vincent in February, we had been
forced to withdraw from the Mediterranean and apart from
a small squadron based at Gibraltar had abandoned it to the
French.

In the North Sea things were little better. The Dutch had
allied themselves with the French and their considerable
fleet based at Texel now threatened to land a large force of
French and Dutch troops in Ireland to support Wolf Tone
and his Irish rebels. To add to our woes there had been a
mutiny in the Channel fleet at Spithead in April which had
spread to the Nore.

This had eventually been settled and the ringleaders
pardoned. However there was still disquiet amongst the
officers at Yarmouth for fear this malady should spread to

us. Things came to a head on 13th of May when the crew of the *Adamant* refused to obey orders.

Now Old Admiral Duncan was a humane man and no martinet but he would not brook such behaviour in his fleet.

"Come with me, Jamie," he cried when he heard the news. "We'll go and see an end to this mischief."

We swiftly crossed to the *Adamant* and soon stood facing the mutineers. The Admiral addressed them sternly. "My lads, while I would rather incur your love than your hate, I am not the least apprehensive of any violent measures you may have in mind. And I tell you straight I will put to death with my own hand any man who shows the least sign of rebellious conduct."

I watched the mutineers with some concern and kept my hand close to the loaded pistol I had in my belt. The Admiral, however, showed not the least apprehension. There was a pause and much muttering amongst the seamen.

The Admiral continued: "Is there any man amongst you who would dispute my command of this fleet, or that of any officer?"

One of the ring leaders stepped forward and cried, "I do!"

Now I should tell you that Admiral Duncan at this time was a man above sixty years of age but of large stature and strongly built. With a cry of rage he rushed forward and taking the man by his shirt carried him to the side of the ship and hung him over. "This is what I think of a fellow who dares to deprive me of my command!" he cried.

I believe he was in such a rage that had not the Chaplain restrained him he would have thrown the fellow overboard. At any rate his bold action resolved the matter for the moment and the crew of the *Adamant* returned to their duty. However the problem was not over and there was considerable unrest throughout the fleet for the next several days although no outright mutiny.

On the 24th May the order came from the Admiralty that the Dutch fleet were about to put to sea and we were ordered to intercept them. On the 29th we raised the signal to weigh anchor and set sail for Texel. This is when the full extent of the unrest became evident.

Most of the crews refused to sail. They took command of the ships from the officers and confined them below decks. The Admiral was black with rage but could do nothing about it and despite renewed signals only two other ships, the 50 gun *Adamant* and the 28 gun frigate *Circe*, joined us in putting to sea. Eventually the admiral regained his composure and signalled the two ships to accompany us eastwards towards the Dutch coast.

As we stood on the quarter deck, still watching the anchored fleet recede in the distance, I ventured a question.

"What are we to do sir, without the fleet?"

"Do Jamie? Why, we will do our duty." And with that remark the Admiral went below deck.

I looked at the lieutenant of the watch who had overheard my question and he shrugged. "The bigger the odds the greater the glory," he said laconically.

"How many ships does De Winter have at Texel?" I asked.

"At the last count he had fifteen or sixteen 74s and half as many frigates."

"Well, there's plenty of glory there," I said with as much bravado as I could muster although in truth I viewed the prospect with some alarm.

It took us four days to come within sight of the Dutch coast. Each day I scanned the western horizon hoping to see the sails of our missing ships but none appeared. Soon we were lying off the outer buoy of the Texel sandbank with the whole Dutch fleet in plain view.

I should explain to those who are not familiar with the area that Texel is a large island off the Dutch coast and some distance out from its western shore lies a long sand bank. The channel between the island and the sandbank provides a secure sheltered anchorage where the Dutch fleet now lay.

My heart sank as I counted the Dutch vessels. There were over fifty. Many of course were transports for the army but there were over a dozen 74s and eight or ten frigates: a formidable fleet and we but three! The Admiral, however, seemed unperturbed and that morning called a conference of the officers of our three ships.

"Well, gentlemen, we have taken up station as ordered and we see before us the might of Holland. Our orders are plain and simple. We are to keep watch over this Dutch fleet and confront and destroy them if they venture forth."

There was an uneasy silence but no one ventured the

obvious question.

The Admiral smiled at them benevolently and continued. "This is what we shall do." He turned to Lieutenant Masters who commanded the *Circe*. "The *Circe* will take up a position hull down on the western horizon with your topmasts in plain view from here."

Masters looked surprised but agreed without demur.

"Meanwhile *Venerable* and *Adamant* will cruise just off shore and keep watch on the Dutch fleet as ordered, and we will regularly signal to you, Lieutenant Masterton, details of their dispositions and such other information as may be of use."

"Yes sir," said Masterton, looking slightly puzzled.

"And you will repeat these signals to the rest of the fleet."

"The rest of the fleet," said Masterton slowly. "But, sir, there is no fleet."

"Ah, my dear sir," said the Admiral with a smile, "you know there is no fleet, and I know there is no fleet, but Admiral De Winter does not. You will be signalling to the fleet that De Winter cannot see, but which is just over the horizon and waiting to pounce upon him should he be so foolish as to venture out."

There was a moment of silence round the table while this statement was digested, then a burst of laughter.

"But will it work?" asked Captain Hotham of the *Adamant* when the laughter had died.

"For that we must wait and see," replied the Admiral. "But

consider this, gentlemen. De Winter will know my flag and the name of *Venerable* is clearly visible to him, and I have little doubt he knows what strength I commanded at Yarmouth."

There was a general murmur of agreement from those around the table. The Dutch like ourselves had many spies amongst the neutral seamen who regularly plied the North Sea.

"Now is it not inconceivable that an old Scotch fool like me would sail all this way to confront his mighty fleet with a mere three ships?"

There were some smiles at this remark.

"If he thinks you a fool, sir, he is sadly in error," said Masterton earnestly.

"Thank you, Mr Masterton," said the Admiral graciously. "But in any event I suspect he may delay his departure at least for a few days until he is more certain of the situation."

It was, of course, a great gamble, but even a few more days delay could allow the rest of our fleet to arrive. No one raised the question of what we would do if the bluff did not work and De Winter came out to confront us. I suppose there was little choice: we either fought or we ran and I did not think the Admiral would be for running.

In the event De Winter did not venture out, and for the next week we cruised close in shore exchanging signals with our distant Frigate who repeated them faithfully to the phantom fleet beyond the horizon. On the morning of the eighth day two sail were sighted approaching from the west and by the 10th of June the full fleet rejoined us.

"Well Jamie," said the Admiral as we stood on the quarter deck of the *Venerable* surveying the assembled ships. "Now we only have one problem."

"What might that be, Sir?"

"Why we have spent the last week trying to persuade De Winter to stay in harbour, and now we must try to persuade him to leave so that we can give him a good trouncing."

I stared across the wide sand bar that separated us from the Dutch fleet. "I doubt he will make such an attempt with us sitting here, Sir. The entrance through the sandbar is only wide enough for one ship at a time to come out and they would be within range of our guns for most of the way."

"Yes, De Winter is safe enough behind his sandbank and I doubt if he will try to break out so long as we remain here," agreed the Admiral.

"Indeed, sir, he is like a mouse in a wine bottle with a cat outside. The cat can see him but cannot reach him, but if he ventures out..."

I was rather pleased with the simile. The Admiral seemed to like it too.

"A very apt description, Jamie, yes, a mouse in a bottle, to be sure." He paused and added almost to himself. "Even quite a small cat could guard the mouth of such a bottle." Then nodding his head in satisfaction and tucking his glass under his arm he went to his cabin.

As I stared after his departing figure, it occurred to me that perhaps his bluff had not been quite so rash after all.

Dundee   end of 1820

THE SPORTING LIFE

Ed Thompson

I was wakened by Molly's hand creeping furtively about
under the pillow. I kept my eyes closed, breathing slowly as
I tried to hold back laughter: that she should try to steal
from me, of all people! *Me?* Her fingers moved again, the
nails catching on the coarse linen. I opened my eyes and
looked at her.

"It's no' there, Molly."

"Wha'?" she slurred, feigning a slow awakening. I rolled
over, trapping her arm.

"It's no' there, Molly," I repeated. "My purse, wallet or
as we in the trade cry it, my *lil* – ye'll no' find it under the
bolster."

"Davy, man, I was just stretchin', honest."

"I'll stretch you!" I said, then moved further across her.
She was morning-warm, soft. "Carry on like that and you'll
be for a seven-year stretch in New South Wales, if they don't
stretch your neck."

"O Davy!" she sighed, spreading herself, changing the
subject.

Yet my mind was not entirely on Molly. If she had found my

40

purse, she would have found it thin. The pleasures of the past few days had used up most of what I had made in Perth. I chanced to be there when the news came that the Queen had been acquitted of adultery, and there was a week of fireworks and balls, with toasts to the health of Queen Caroline, and damnation to King George. A full week of opportunities to collect watches, lift wallets, and roll drunks.

Well, the money from all that was gone. No more brandy and flash women – *blones,* as we call them – like Molly here. No more visits to the Theatre Royal in Castle Street to sit in the fine red plush seats jeering at the actors and admiring the actresses' bubbies. It was time for me to get back to work and earn a living.

Hearing the waterman's cart from one of the town wells clattering along outside, I called for a pitcher of hot water, and when it came washed my face, oxters and fork with care. If you are to move among the quality, it does not do to stink like one of their servants. Molly declined my offer of a share, save for a quick splash under her shift. No doubt she knew her own business best. Many men would take pleasure in the musk of her body, and I had made it plain that our time together was over. She must be about her work too, and find someone else to keep her.

During our time in Dundee I had of course kept my eyes open. In the arcade under the Town House – 'The Pillars' as it is called – there was a jeweller's shop whose little bow windows held a rare show of watches. A little further along the High Street I noticed another jeweller, William Constable. Not a name that appealed to me. However it was time now to take a more serious prospect of the town. So out into the Nethergate I went, a shawl over my shoulder and a great Scots bonnet hiding my face. As long as I kept my mouth wide open I would be taken for a country bumpkin, and would be expected to gape at everything around me.

To the west, along the Perth Road, were the grand houses of the gentry, each with its gate giving on to the river. Many had a fanlight over the front door, an arrangement which almost invites an active man to slip in at night. But the reward for this is uncertain and – I know not why – I crave the excitement of more personal sport, as well as the money. I would much prefer to pluck some rich, young laird with a taste for brandy and cards; but I could not wait for the kind of market or fair that brings these empty-headed noodles out in their droves.

For my taste there were altogether too many bookshops in Dundee, their windows filled with bound sermons and improving tracts. In the Nethergate itself there were schools for the sons of the burgesses, and teachers of drawing and dancing for their daughters. There were too many businesses connected with the linen trade, or fishing for whales; too many insurance companies and banks. There is wealth there, no doubt, but not enough loose cash. The trouble with Dundee, I saw, was that the persons most fit to be robbed generally sauntered about in small groups between Morrow's Hotel and the Trades Hall, where there was a subscription reading room. Or they stood in twos or threes to discuss the news of the day. What is worse, they were mostly sober. To ply my art, I needed to have them standing crowded close together, and preferably flown with drink.

Then I saw how with care and preparation something might be contrived, and I circled round Dundee once again, an honest countryman in my homespuns. This time I was marking distances and times in my head, and studying most carefully the condition of the streets and pends along which I would make my run. Constable's jewellery shop was conveniently close to Tindal's Wynd, but the High Street itself was too broad. The arcade under the Town House would be better, for there was less space and less light, and the pillars would hinder movement. As I made my way past the shop windows here, I glanced out of the corner of my eye at the watches, noting the position of the gold ones. The smell of fresh leather was strong under the arches, from a boot shop and a saddler that stood beside yet another bookshop

I stepped down on to the High Street and wandered over towards the mercat cross. The whores penned up on the top floor of the Town House were hanging out of the prison windows calling to the passers-by: *Haw! Mistress Doig! I was wi' yer man yestre'en. No muckle in his breeches pocket noo, eh? Nor in his breeches, neither!* They howled at their own wit, and their irreverent spirit cheered me. I used some of my remaining money bribing a turnkey to take them up a bottle of gin, doffing my bonnet and waving to be sure they would recognise me again.

Then it was along the High Street once more, dodging a couple of Mr Macintosh's chairmen, carrying one of the great dames of the town about her business. The men had the usual heavy shoulders and thick calves of their trade, beasts of burden fit to trot about town all day carrying the ladies in their rented sedan chairs; but they had not the speed to worry me if it came to a chase. There were carts and baskets belonging to the farmers' wives who had come in to sell their eggs and chickens, vegetables, butter and cheese, but they would be no obstacle either. Indeed the litter of their discarded rubbish that lay over the cobbles, with fallen leaves and horse droppings, would simply serve to impede any dainty pursuer who came running after me. The crossing man who swept the street outside the coaching inn was a cripple, and the ballad singer by the mercat cross was an old soldier, judging by his faded red coat. He had lost a leg, or had it tied up out of sight, and would not trouble me either.

Tindal's Wynd, leading down to the Fishmarket, looked promising: narrow enough to deter any horseman who wished to pursue me, and slightly downhill to give me added speed. Better yet, there were three or four different ways out at the end. The market area itself was treacherous underfoot, with its discarded fish guts, but I would not expect to be still pursued as I skirted it.

Finally I went down to Mary Kidd's place, she being the dealer I had used to fence the watches, chains and masonic trinkets that had come my way in Perth. Mary agreed to have a smart lad standing at the foot of the wynd when I wanted. He would take the loot from the jeweller's as I passed. I asked to see him, of course, since my neck would be in his hands. He was a thin, quick, barefoot, red-haired rogue, much as I myself had been ten years before. I gave him a shilling, then added another when he suggested improvements in my proposed route.

Mary also directed me to an old-clothes dealer, a discreet man who asked no questions but supplied me on her account with a set of dark garments which would give me the appearance of a sailor. No-one would be surprised if they saw me coming up from the direction of the Fishmarket carrying a box on my shoulder. Mary arranged this too. My countryman's homespuns went into a simple valise. My preparations were almost complete.

Walking slowly towards The Pillars, looking around carefully at the position of the people in the High Street, I slipped on the brass knuckles I always carry. My fingers are important to my profession, and I would not wish to damage them if I had to hit someone. This time, though, the knuckles were simply to deal with the window.

As I came alongside the jeweller's I drove my fist through a small pane of glass. It was the work of an instant to reach in and seize the gold watch and two of its lesser neighbours, then leap across the paved area outside the shop and start my run along the High Street. I swerved round a group of gossiping farmers' wives, dodged past a couple of chairmen, and ran on.

The shouting behind me began and I was dismayed to hear the sound of someone making good speed over the cobbles. When I glanced back I saw a young soldier, an ensign or the like from the garrison at Dudhope Castle, who was at least keeping pace with me. I shifted my grip on the knuckleduster and was preparing to break his jaw for him when I heard a shriek from above, and something like a mortar bomb or grenade exploded in front of the redcoat. I could not but look back, and saw him halted in a spray of glass and liquid, evidently from a bottle thrown down from the town jail. A gin bottle, I would judge, and not filled with water either. It was followed by the rest of a chamberpot, emptied with howls of glee by the whores above.

Gardyloo! I called back over my shoulder, laughing as I raced on in the direction of the Seagate, then I jouked like a hare to my right and darted into Tindal's Wynd, which leads down towards the harbour. The crossing sweeper who stood leaning on his broom outside the Trades Hall may have seen which way I had gone, but most of the folk in the High Street had been distracted by the exchange of insults being shouted back and forth between the soldier and the doxies.

Down through Tindal's Wynd I ran, a narrow lane and lively enough, with at least one bousing ken among its big houses. It was fairly busy, but with folk who knew better than to hinder a man in a hurry. At the foot of the lane Mary Kidd's boy waited, seated on a wooden fish box at the corner. He stood as I approached.

We collided, and the watches disappeared into his shirt while I swung the box up and on to my shoulder. When I looked round he had gone, and I now trudged on towards the Fishmarket at the steady pace of a man who does this all day long.

Then it was down into Fish Street – which they called the *Holy Land*, being a fine lawless place at night – and up Couttie's Wynd, the box on my shoulder concealing my face. Of course I had little to fear now, having nothing of the jeweller's in my possession, but I had no wish to be delayed.

Arrived back at the Nethergate I was soon into my lodgings where I quickly threw on my white topcoat and tall hat, picked up my dog-whip with its lead-filled handle, and returned to the Nethergate with the languid gait of the sportsman.

I sauntered idly along past the English Chapel, where the coopers and their apprentices stood by their casks and barrels, staring towards the Town House. A satisfactory crowd was streaming towards the Pillars. The jeweller was outside his shop expostulating on the gang of villains who had robbed him of a number of fine gold watches, though I knew it was but one villain and only one gold watch. I pushed my way through the townsfolk who were jammed into the arcade, crowded together as I had hoped. Now the fox was at last among the geese.

"Surely the villain must have cut himself on that?" I cried, as I rapped with my dog-whip on the shop window beside the shards of broken glass, and of course all heads turned to follow my tapping whip and study the damage. As they bent to search for drops of blood my other hand was instantly at work, teasing out wallets and pocketbooks. I had three likely ones in a minute or two, chosen for their weight and thickness. I had to move quickly, not having a partner to take off my prizes, but still for mere sport I relieved a swag-bellied burgess of his watch, chain and seals in a single move – and placed them gently in the coat pocket of his neighbour. It was one of those Spencer coats that fashionable members of the town council were wearing on top of their overcoats that season, and the pockets hung open of themselves. I added a silk handkerchief (a *sleek wipe*, as we would say) which I snibbed from another of his neighbours, this time leaving it drooping from his pocket in plain view.

Then I worked my way back through the crowd and strolled off towards the harbour, as though to see in which direction the thieving sailor had gone. As I did so I turned the dog-whip round, reversing the handle and putting the weighted part into position to serve as a bludgeon if need be. I was in no mind to be stopped now.

I was turning into Castle Street when I heard an altercation beginning behind me. The geese were beginning to honk at each other! Just past the theatre the red-headed lad appeared at my elbow, guiding me up a narrow pend to the right – Doig's Close, I think it was called. Mrs Kidd and I had business to transact.

The boy led me through a maze of narrow passageways and into a room where Mary sat at a table. She gave me the chair which placed my back to the wall, a sure sign that she had someone close by if she needed help. I emptied the coins out of the pocketbooks I had taken, making two piles. One I passed to the boy, bidding him scout around the town to see where the constables were.

After he had left the room I opened the pocket-books: one contained fifteen pounds in British Linen Bank notes. Another held some boys from the Dundee Bank, along with a gold seal; the third was a cheat, stuffed with scraps of paper. Mary produced the watches I had lifted, laid them between us on the table: "Twal pun' for the gowd," she said, "five for the ither twa thegither."

I touched the gold watch. "The *dross scout* here," I said, "is worth mair than twal. Gie me yer note for twinty, an' ye can hae them aa'." I threw the seal down to join the watches. "And ye can hae the *scut* for a luckpenny."

Mary paused, then nodded. Really we were dickering for form's sake only. I gladly accepted the notes and folded them tightly into a long strip. A touch of my penknife opened the seam at the side of my collar, and I replaced the stiffening in it with the folded banknotes. Just then the boy returned, laughing merrily as he told us that the constables were busy dealing with the fights that had broken out in the High Street. There was talk of reading the Riot Act but I would have no difficulty boarding the ferry.

"If ye've a fancy for the sporting life," I said to him as I left, "look for me in the Grassmarket. They'll ken whaur tae find me."

"Gin ye hivnae been hangit," Mary added.

"Aye," I agreed. "We're all like tae end on the gallows. But a man will live and tak some pleasure first."

Down Castle Street I went for the last time, then along in the gloaming to the Craig pier to board the new *Union* paddle steamer just as she was about to leave on the last passage of the day. There was no livestock on board for this sailing so the outer hulls of the ferry were empty, and few passengers in the centre beside the paddle wheel. By some mechanical ingenuity the paddle was made to turn backwards, so the ferry sailed straight back out from the pier, before turning round in the river. Then the master stopped and let the ferry drift on round, before throwing it into its proper motion, which sent us surging away across towards Newport.

I stood at the stern of the *Union*, looking back over the foam thrown up by the paddle. Upriver, towards Perth, the sky was a blaze of orange and yellow where the sun was setting; in the other direction, towards Broughty Ferry and the German Ocean, it was already dark. There could be no pursuit now. It would be a fine night.

GLEANERS OF NATURE

Ann Prescott

Round the corner, Overgate Street was not much better. Between heaps of snow, splashed with mud and worse, a brown trail snaked down towards the Luckenbooths. The mish-mash of old houses and new tenements had lost their familiar identities. To Elisabeth Smith they loomed in on her like grey spectres. She squelched to a new tenement on the North side and stamped up the spiral stair-well at the back of the close. The acrid sting of damp soot caught her throat and brought on a fit of coughing so, by the time she reached the landing, Ma already had the door open.

In an instant she was in the snug living room, its warm close atmosphere offering comforting overtones of mutton broth. Mary and Chick clamoured round her as usual until Ma shooed them away, telling them to let their sister get rid of her wet clothes before pestering her. The bairns retreated. Her frozen fingers fumbled with buttons and ties and soon skirt and petticoats had joined her outer garments on the clothes' horse in front of the range and she was crouched before the fire. As yet unseen by his elders Chick began to make rivers of melted snow on the oil-cloth floor covering.

Eliza knew she could delay no longer. "I've quit, Ma,"

she blurted out. "I'm not going back. I'm not!" She burst into tears.

Mrs Smith's attention was on the glass chimney that she was carefully rotating over the flame of the oil lamp, newly lit although it was barely 4 o'clock. She allowed her hand to stray too close to the heat and was betrayed into exclaiming, "Scissors!" before enquiring of her daughter whatever had brought this on?

Gradually the story emerged. Miss McEwen had always hated her. She'd been pick, pick, pick. Miss McEwen accused her of getting a spot of blood on a chemise. The gas pressure was so low that there had been scarce a glimmer of light. It would have been no wonder if she had pricked her finger. "But it wasn't me, Ma. She docked my wages, Ma. It wasn't fair." Eliza's sobs began afresh.

Mrs Smith did not attempt to stem her daughter's catalogue of woes. She had assembled the lamp and now turned up the wick. Leaning across the table she patted Eliza on the shoulder. "What's done is done. Your Father would go down to the Harbour despite his leg. He'll be worn out when he returns so put on your pretty face for him and we'll say naught of this until we have resolved matters."

The blizzard raged all week. Dundee was completely cut off until Sunday when a coach and six horses managed to get through with the London mail. Mr Smith was the only one of his family to venture outdoors, ostensibly to offer his assistance to the Harbour Manager and to bring in a few necessities. His wife and elder daughter were well aware that he would sooner lose both legs than miss his visits to the Exchange Reading Rooms and Coffee House.

Pondering on her daughter's plight Mrs Smith came up with a notion. She happened to know that George Robertson, who kept a genteel shop on the south side, was extending his business and required a lady assistant, Mrs Robertson being in a delicate condition. Eliza was well-suited for such a position. Eliza herself was less certain. Seeing in her face her daughter's proper reluctance to put herself forward, Mrs Smith mentioned that there would be time to make over the puce pelisse that she had grown too jolly to wear and that Eliza could trim her bonnet to match.

So, on Monday morning, Eliza fastened the bonnet over her neatly braided hair, took a last critical look at her reflection in the brass base of the lamp, received a kiss from her Mother and crossed the street to enter the Castle of Otranto. The cheerful tinkle of the doorbell alerted Mr Robertson to his early caller. Blushing furiously, Eliza stammered out her mission. There was a moment's heart-stopping silence. Then Mr Robertson laid the tips of his fingers together and offered her a month's trial without wages. "Subject to Mrs Robertson's approval," he added hastily, noting her trim figure.

Besides Mr Robertson, the establishment consisted of the Boy, who ran errands, Molly Docherty, who came in twice a day to do the regular cleaning, and Mr Gardiner, who worked in the back premises manufacturing and repairing the umbrellas that were the main item of stock. This season much of the umbrella trade involved replacing the heavy alpaca covers of the wood and whalebone "thunder-sticks" which had an unfortunate tendency to shrink to grotesque shapes as they dried.

Mr Gardiner was a slight, wiry man about Eliza's own height. She thought he must be quite old, twenty at least. Eliza became familiar with the treasure trove of hose and gloves that filled the long, shallow drawers under the counter. "A place for everything," she told her Mother. She enjoyed fulfilling the customers' requirements and was proud when Mr Robertson left her in sole charge when he went to the Trades Hall for his daily dose of politics.

According to the "Advertiser" six thousand men, representing the majority of the adult male population of the town, had signed the petition demanding that the Government undertook revision of the electoral process. Ask any woman, however, high or low, old or young, and she would instantly affirm that the entire adult male population was besotted with and obsessed by the topic of electoral reform. Eliza's own Mother was wont to vent her exasperation at this display of masculine single-mindedness by declaring that for 25 shillings a week she would run the country herself.

The morning that Eliza was to remember for the rest of her life began during one of Mr Robertson's absences. Jimmy

Mudie's handcart scraped to a halt outside the shop and Jimmy kicked open the door and thumped a large parcel on the polished counter.

"Stockings from Mrs Morris," he announced. "That'll be a penny ha'penny, Eliza."

"Miss Eliza to you, Jimmy Mudie." She opened the till and counted the coppers into his palm.

Intent on preventing Jimmy from 'borrowing' anything not nailed down, she came from behind the counter and held open the door for him before tackling the package. Using her small silver scissors to tease the twine, she undid the knots before starting on the cloth wrappings. Then she screamed.

Someone rushed from the back premises. "Miss Smith! Are you hurt?"

Eliza pointed to the package. A golden-brown insect had emerged from the coverings and was preparing to dart across the counter straight at her!

"A gollock, an orange gollock!"

To her indignation Mr Gardiner laughed. He extended his finger and the creature obediently crawled on to his wrist.

"Aren't you going to kill it?" she demanded.

"Whatever for?" He peered at his small guest. "She's an earwig. I'll keep her snug in my pocket until I find a safe place for her to lodge."

"An earwig," Eliza repeated, bemused.

"An earwig," gravely echoed Mr Gardiner. "Yet, Miss Smith, these humble creatures have brought me my greatest good fortune." He had caught her astonished attention. "Not that it was evident at the outset," he continued. "When I was a wee bairn my Mother made me empty my pockets." He raised his voice a pitch. "'Hang the laddie, he wid hae his snails and horn gollocks creeping' a' owre the hoose gin I would let him.' My mentor – my uncle - chanced to be present. He saved me from a skelping. Far more, from that moment, he stimulated and assisted me in attaining knowledge of the glories of God's visible creation. With his encouragement I joined the Gleaners of Nature and now enjoy the companionship of like-minded souls."

When Eliza regaled her Mother with this queer tale of an *earwig* Mrs Smith said tartly that Maggie Gardiner had always been something of a shrew and her husband was too fond of the two-handed crack with his cronies to pay any heed to his bairns. The story went that William had been mending china for Mr Barclay up the Westport when he was barely seven. A year or two later David Barclay took him on as apprentice to the umbrella trade. The lad would have had little chance of schooling were it not for his Uncle's intervention.

"Douglas Gardiner?" interjected Mr Smith, entering the room at the end of the conversation. "Didn't he have a botanic garden overlooking the old Windmill Brae? He was Superintendent of the Museum of the Rational Institute that was sold off some ten years ago. My old Father would often quote him: 'Knowledge is the best worldly solace under the ills of life and its most powerful engine to overcome them.'"

On the first Monday in April, about two months after Eliza had begun her new employment, Dundee celebrated in style. Eliza had been taken on by Mr Robertson at a wage of six shillings per week and the House of Commons had voted by a majority of one in favour of the Reform Bill! The Provost and Councillors decreed that there should be a Grand Illumination.

In the late afternoon Father hoisted Chick on to his shoulders and, with his wife on one arm and Eliza on the other, they strolled towards the Harbour. The upper floor of the Trades Hall, at the east end of the High Street, was ablaze with light. Mary skipped round them like a little tug boat until the noise of squibs sent her close to Mrs Smith's side. A veritable explosion of noise welcomed them at the end of Castle Street as the vessels, bedecked with flags, sounded their minute guns.

Eliza stood enraptured, gazing at the tracery of moonlight on the Tay and, rising from the blackness beyond, the hills of Fife radiant with fire. When they turned to retrace their steps the lights from the town eclipsed the bright moon! As the family paused to admire the spectacle Eliza observed William Gardiner walking alone and something about the solitary figure made her beckon him over. Mr Smith invited him to join them and Mrs Smith reinforced the invitation with the request that he returned with them for a bite of supper and a sing-song as nobody would get much sleep that night.

April turned out to be a blustery month. "Good for trade,"

said Mr Robertson. To the envy of all her girl friends Eliza accompanied him to the preview of summer stock at Haldane's in Castle Street and was delighted to be allowed to choose the ginghams for the parasols and light umbrellas. She and William Gardiner passed some agreeable hours deciding on the ways to cut the cloth to best advantage. She discovered then that, whereas William's body might inhabit the confines of the shop, his spirit roamed free in his beloved Forfarshire countryside. Towards the end of the month, when the weather was picking up, he invited her to accompany him on a Sunday ramble to experience this pleasure herself.

Her parents willingly gave their sanction. Little Mary, drinking in every word, danced round the room chanting, "Liza's got a beau!" until Eliza was forced to beg Ma make her stop. But she was not displeased. She informed her friends that she would not be joining them for their customary promenade and felt a sense of adventure when they teased her about her preference for 'traipsing in mud'.

So it was with eager anticipation that she met William after morning service and set off with him up the Scouring Burn. It was a perfect day. As they left behind the brooding steam mills Eliza removed her bonnet and lifted her voice in 'All hail the power of Jesus' name'. William's tenor joined her soprano and, in no time at all, they were climbing the wooded slopes of Balgay.

William showed her a patch of rare cowslips blooming among the pines in the hollow that divided the Hill in the middle. In Eliza's opinion their sweet, delicate fragrance surpassed that of every plant she knew. When they reached Tay Grove he named shepherd's purse, lemon celandine, borage, ivy-leaved speedwell, purple archangel, coltsfoot and corn violet. Eliza retaliated by challenging him to identify her bonnet. "Tuscany, Dunstable, Straw or Italian Straw?" she demanded. He was completely nonplussed until he saw her bright eyes and cried out, "Miss Elizabeth, you're teasing me!"

Monday morning got off to a bad start. Eliza didn't wake until she was roused by the six o'clock peal of town bells and, horror, the clatter of the night-soil cart. She scrambled into her robe, grabbed the receptacles, and rushed down to the street. The summer flock of half-naked, bare-footed bairns jeered at her disarray until Mr Andrews opposite, attired in leather apron and shirt sleeves, chased them off. Eliza had eagerly anticipated going over yesterday's events with William but to her infinite frustration Mr Robertson had jobs that detained her for several hours.

When eventually she picked up a heap of covers and went into the back premises her eyes took seconds to adjust to the darkness. With its racks of wooden shafts and sheets of baleen stacked against the mildewed wallpaper the space couldn't be more depressing. William was occupied adjusting stretchers at his work bench, and for some seconds was completely oblivious of her presence. When he did speak it was as though he were resuming a conversation. "My Father entrusted me to prepare the summer programme of Sabbath rambles for the Gleaners. I believe I have now devised excursions that will satisfy the diverse interests of all the members."

She wondered whether this meant their walks were at an end. Still following his own train of thought, William misinterpreted her silence and went on, "My Father considered me a ne'er do well until he heard me speak on *The Tenacity of Life Displayed by the Earwig* at one of our monthly gatherings. For the first time he met his discarded son on a common platform and, to my infinite pleasure, has become my good companion ever since."

Eliza laid the covers on the work bench and, with a flounce of her wide skirt, returned to the shop. She was not sure he noticed her go.

Yet Eliza was not forgotten. At midday William laid before her a promised sheet of elegantly mounted dried flowers collected during the previous season. Eliza nobly put her chagrin behind her and afforded them the admiration they deserved. She even begged to be instructed in the art of preservation. The upshot was that on the evening of the Sabbath following William arrived at her parents' house with the plants he had collected that day, a package of blotting paper, an English pencil, and a posy of wild flowers for Eliza.

Seated around the table the family watched as he instructed Eliza how to arrange a bloom to best advantage on a square of blotting paper and cover it with a second sheet marked with its name, location, and date of collection in his own

Ann Prescott

meticulous hand. When all were assembled to his satisfaction, with Mrs Smith's bemused permission, he laid them under the oil-cloth at the door and requested that they be left undisturbed for a month. Eying him sternly Eliza trusted that Chick was paying heed.

Whilst the women prepared a light supper, Mr Smith, who had learnt that William had attended Dr Dick's lecture on the properties of the atmosphere, sought his view on Dr Franklin's hypothesis that the *Aurora Borealis,* so spectacular that year, were caused by electrical fluid escaping into the upper atmosphere of the polar regions. Eliza was delighted with the approbation William received from her family; the more so when the evening ended with a recitation of his poem entitled 'The Laced-winged Fly', a performance that won universal acclaim.

On July 9th, when the gooseberries were ripe and summer was promising to be long and hot and trying, Mr Robertson stuck a notice in the window of the shop informing his customers that the Haberdashers, Clothiers, Hatters, Hosiers, and Glovers of the town had agreed to SHUT shop every evening at 8 (Saturdays excepted).

That evening Eliza and William joyfully left behind the stifling streets for an excursion to Will's Braes. The tranquil river flowing past the green hills of Fife had never looked lovelier nor had the birds sung more sweetly. Swinging her bonnet by its strings, Eliza stood on the narrow path that separated the Braes from the cornfields to the north and breathed a deep lungful of the clean, tangy air. The low sun gleamed on her dark braids. Glancing back at her William exclaimed, "You're like a beautiful blackbird. Your dress, the soft blue of her eggs and your hair...." For once at a loss for words he broke off, his pale face flushing. "I beg your pardon, Miss Elizabeth."

Eliza held out her hands, "William," she said, "you.... you great gollock!"

On July 13th, 1834, William Gardiner sent a note to Miss E R Smith addressed to "My Dearest Eliza" and signed "Your ever faithful lover." He included a poem the closing lines of which read:

> *An the sunshine o' love sparkles aye in her ee*
> *For her young fond heart is as leal to me*
> *As the bird to her mate on the white haw-tree*
> *And the dearest wish that I e're did feel*
> *Is to wish that her heart may ever be leal.*

DEAD ED

Gill Blackmore

His name is Ed. And he's my best pal. And he's dead. He's not a ghost; Ed says ghosts are for children's stories and Halloween. They're not like in real life, or real death. It's plain and simple. He was Ed. Now he's dead. So he's Dead Ed.

I've known him for ages. I can't remember the first time I seen him. He's just been there all my life. He says he used to sing to me when I was a baby 'cos he got sick to the back teeth of all my bawling. I was a right wee pain, Dead Ed says, when I was young. I'm nine now, same as him, so we're best pals.

The first thing I remember about Dead Ed was when I was five years old. He'd be waiting for me when I come home from school and play with me till I went to bed. Well I'm not allowed out much 'cos of my bad chest. I take inhalers and everything but mum still worries. She wants to move away from here cos she thinks the cold sea air is bad for me. But dad says East Haven has been his family's home for generations and he's not budging. I don't want to move either. I'd miss Dead Ed.

I even miss him when I go to school. Dead Ed says I'm lucky. He only got to go to school for three years. Then he had to help his dad with the fishing. He loved school and he rolls his eyes and spits if I tell him I hate it. Then he tells me stories of how hard it was for him and his family when they lived in my house. I wouldn't tell Dead Ed 'cos I think he'd be angry, but I like it when he tells me his stories, 'specially the bits about the yucky stuff. Like they didn't have toilets and had to pee and poo outside in a small hut and when the bucket was full they took it down to the beach and threw it in the sea. Gross.

Dead Ed says I have it easy. But at least he didn't have homework and he never had to take horrible medicines. He never even saw a doctor. Not in his whole life. Not even when he was dying of the Scarlet Fever. His family couldn't afford one. When I told him that doctors were free now, his eyes nearly rolled out of their sockets and he spat three times in a row. He says I don't know I'm living, which I think is a funny thing for a dead person to say.

Anyway, today Dead Ed told me some awesome news. Tonight I can travel back in time with him to when he was alive. We're going back to 1848, which is over 150 years ago! We have to go tonight, cos it's just before my tenth birthday. After that, I will be older than Dead Ed was when he died and I can never see him again. That's the sad part but I'm not thinking about it 'cos Dead Ed says it can't be changed; dead people can't be seen by people who are older than they were when they died. He doesn't know why, it's just one of them things. Like when you get sore wind after eating beans.

But I'm not sure if I believe Dead Ed. It would be great

if it *is* true. But I'm not sure I believe all of his stories. I mean he told me that his dad was a fisherman and when he went out to sea, his mum carried him out to his boat on her back, to save his dad being wet on the long fishing trip. He got annoyed when I burst out laughing. He said it wasn't funny for all the poor lassies who had to do it for their menfolk. But I just couldn't picture my mum doing that for my dad. He'd flatten her.

But if we do go, I don't want to stand out too much. Dead Ed's clothes are a bit different to mine, but he says I can borrow his bunnet and neckertie and I can just wear my white school shirt and grey trousers. Dead Ed says he can roll me in some muck when we get there and make it more realistic 'cos no one looked as clean as me back then. That's another good thing about when Dead Ed was alive. They didn't have baths.

Dead Ed's coming to get me on the first stroke of midnight. I couldn't eat my tea. Mum sent me to bed 'cos she thinks I'm sickening for something. I wish I could tell her. I wish I could tell someone.

I must have fallen asleep 'cos suddenly Dead Ed's hissing in my ear, "Wake up, wake up, lad. It's time. We maun hurry."

"Hi Dead Ed. It's okay, I'm dressed. I didn't get changed into my pyjamas to save time."

"Good thinking, but you maun hasten alang. I've never done this afore and I'm no sure aboot it. I mean, I ken the rules, I learnt them aff your great grandfather. He had the gift, like you. But he got feart at the last minute."

A cold squeeze in my stomach makes me gulp like I've swallowed icy lemonade too fast.

"Did he not go then? Maybe I shouldn't...."

"Dinnae you tak cauld feet. He was a right snivelling bairn. No like you. Come on, you're no gonnae give up the greatest adventure of yer life, are you? You're aye telling me what a boring time it is, cooped up here. You hae to break awa fae your ma's pinny strings sometime, laddie."

Dead Ed's always called me lad or laddie. I never minded before when I was younger, but now I wish he'd call me by my name sometimes, like real best pals do.

"Okay I'll do it. But it'll be alright, won't it, Dead Ed?"

"Course. But dinnae forget, lad. Dinnae be calling me Dead Ed when we get there. I'll be Ed. Plain and simple."

Then Dead Ed takes me downstairs. With only a dim night-light on in the hall the house feels strange. Like it's holding its breath. I'm holding mine too when I creep over the one creaky step on our stairs. I try to let a breath out quietly but it still makes a bit of a wheeze. Mum's a light sleeper cos she always listens out for my bad breathing. I stop to hear if she stirs but Dead Ed is waving frantically at me. I go as fast as I can on my tiptoes down the last few steps and follow him through to the kitchen. He's standing beside the door to where the washing machine is.

"Switch the light aff, ye idiot."

I hadn't realised I'd switched it on. The sudden darkness is horrible. I can't see Dead Ed and his voice makes me shiver. All I want now is to be back safe in my bed.

"Right then lad, walk through this door wi' me and we can go back in time. We cannae git there less we go thegither. Leave that bit tae me. I ken whit tae dae."

"I don't know about this Dead Ed, maybe…"

Then Dead Ed walks right into my body and suddenly I feel my feet moving. A cold draught catches my breath and I feel my chest close in like it does. Oh no, my inhalers! I forgot them. I try to tell Dead Ed but he ignores me.

The darkness slowly lifts and I'm standing in a small room looking at some people sitting around a fire, a real little bonfire, with real flames and everything. We have a gas fire and mum says it's just like a proper fire, but it's nothing like this, with blackened wood hissing and creaking. And blue flames and white sparks leaping and sizzling. There's a pot hanging down over the fire and it looks like a witch's cauldron. I shiver in the shadows.

Dead Ed walks over to a chair and crooks his finger at me. I take a deep breath, but my legs won't move. I can't get my breath. It's like a furry rug is being held over my nose and mouth and I'm suffocating in a stink of fishy smoke.

"Mither, I've brocht Wattie ower for supper. His ma's no weel," says Dead Ed.

Wattie? Who's Wattie? I look behind me but I'm standing alone. I think he means me. I didn't know this was part of the game.

"Och no' anither wan taen no weel. Poor Flora. She hae a rash, Wattie?"

The lady, Dead Ed's mum, turns to look at me. I nearly faint. She's all crumpled like an old balloon left behind the couch. Her face squishes into a smile and her teeth are yellow with brown bits. She looks like a witch and I glance at the cauldron again. My mouth dries but I take a few shallow breaths and my chest opens up a bit.

"No like you, Wattie, tae hud yer wheesht so. Come ahint and let the fire warm the cockles," Dead Ed's mum says before she turns her face back to the fire. "Mary, go fetch me some mair tatties. Wattie's a fine growin' laddie."

"Aye, mither."

Mary stands up and smiles over at me. I've never seen a lady wear a long skirt like that. And she has a little white apron tied round her waist which she rubs her hands on before tying a floppy white hat under her chin and throwing a little black blanket thing round her shoulders. The fire jumps and leans over with a loud crackle when she closes the door behind her.

"Here Wattie, sit doon here," says Dead Ed, pulling a small wooden three-legged stool close to his chair at the side of the fire. He begins warming his hands and rubbing them over his cheeks. He sighs loudly and stretches out like a cat.

I manage to get the courage to move over to the fireside and sit on the hard little seat, which wobbles a lot and I nearly tip over, which might hurt cos there's no carpet on the floor, just some brown stuff that looks like earth, but surely can't be.

I dare a quick peek at Dead Ed's mum again. She looks

up from the bowl she has on her lap and smiles her squishy smile. A tiny droplet of sweat hangs off her nose. She quickly swipes it away with the back of a hand covered in a rough brown mixture that looks like grainy mud.

'Dinnae look so worried, son. Yer ma doesnae hae the rash. Ken it'll no be yon Scarlet Fever. Mind, it's an ill wind's been blawin' these past days. And noo there's this devil's-breath fog. There'll be some poor cratur taen afore the week's out. May oor Lord see fit to spare the twa bairns he hasnae taen fae me yet. Mibbe yer ma has the richt idea Wattie, sending you awa to yer Great Auntie Jeannie's up Dundee. Tis the morrow you go, eh son? Aye Eddie, I was jist saying tae yer da, yer fair gaein' tae miss him. Nae wan tae git into ony high jinks wi'!' She cackled suddenly and her eyes seemed to disappear into the saggy folds of her face.

"Richt noo, we hae mealy crab and tatties for supper. Whit aboot gieing us wan o' yer songs Wattie? Tae wile awa the time till the tatties boil. You've sich a bonny wee voice."

"They've nae time for ony o' that, Mither," a hoarse voice booms out. A man's big round face comes forward past the sticky out bits at the topsides of his chair. He looks a bit like a dirty Santa Claus with a pipe in his mouth, which he doesn't take out when he speaks.

"Git yer backsides ootside and git to reddin me lines. There's plenty o' bark. I put it there masel' the morn. Yer no needin' tae sing for your supper, you kin work for it instead." He snorts out a laugh and a big cloud of smoke puffs out his nose. He disappears back behind the sides of his chair, so I can only see his legs sticking out at the bottom and smoke blowing out at the top.

"Come on Wattie. There's nae rest for the wicked," sighs Dead Ed standing up and yawning.

"Aye, an' the devil finds work fir the idle," Dead Ed's dad calls out with another snort-laugh. Dead Ed grins. I remember I've got his cap in my pocket and put it on. I like the feel of it on my head. Dead Ed hands me a jacket and puts a cap and jacket on himself. Mary comes in carrying a small bundle of potatoes in her arms, puffing out her cheeks and stamping her feet.

"Feels like bloody winter and we've jist haen oor pare excuse fir a summer an' all," says Mary as she passes us in the doorway.

"I heard that blaspheme Mary Jean Crawford. There'll be nane o' that in this hoose."

"Sorry Ma," says Mary in a sweet voice, rolling her eyes at us and shutting the door.

The cold air hits my chest and I gasp.

"Whit's the matter, laddie? Yer chist agin?" says Dead Ed.

"Yeah, but it's alright Dead...I mean Ed. I just wish I'd brought my inhalers."

"I'll git my ma tae gie you wan o' her brews. She haes wan for a bad chist. Gie's it tae Wattie's ma a' the time. She's got a bad chist too."

"Oh yeah that reminds me, why's everyone calling me Wattie?"

'Because you're back in time. You're noo you're great-great-great grandfather."

"But he's dead."

"No' noo he's no. You're alive and weel, Walter James Herd."

I can hardly take it in. I'm my great-great-great-grandfather? That can't be right.

"Noo, we hae tae boil da's lines for him. I ken you never done ony reddin afore. Yon laddies fae your time never ken nothin' useful. Onyway, we needs tae dae it tae git a' the slime aff the fishin' lines. Git a handfu' o' that bark there and pit it in this pail. Then, we'll boil it up ower here.....hey whit's the maiter, laddie?"

I know I must look a sight cos I never seen Ed's eyes pop out so much. I need my inhaler bad. The last thing I hear is Ed calling my name from far, far away.

I wake up in a kind of camp bed just a little bit off the floor. I try to sit up but I can't lift the weight of my own head. My skin seems to scrape off the cover like I've got hard corners instead of soft skin.

"Hush cheil. Tak yer time. You've had a sorry nicht o' it, but yer ower the worst for noo'. Thanks be to oor Lord God Almichty (an' o'coorse wi the help o' a muckle dollop o' Molly Crawford's special brew) and Amen to that."

The voice is strange but comforting and I lie back again. I don't know how long I slept, but when I woke I could hear voices outside the door.

"He's no weel enough tae travel the day. An' I'm no sure he ever will be. Did ye see the rash tha's come up on his neck? Tis the selfsame wan as on his ma's face. Could be the Scarlet Fever.

Seems tae favour the bairns and the sickly and you ken his ma's never been richt since the sea taen her man last winter."

I've got Scarlet Fever? I don't know what it is but I know it's not good. Dead Ed died of it. Oh God, I've got to get home. I try to sit up but I feel like I'm made of cotton wool now. I try to shout but only a bubble comes out my mouth.

"Hey there laddie, dinnae try tae speak, ye'll tire yersel' oot."

I turn my head slowly.

"Dead Ed, help me. I need to get home." My voice is only a whisper and Dead Ed has to bend down to hear me.

"Ye cannae noo boy. Ye missed the deadline. Yer stuck here. You see laddie, yer too sick wi' yer bad chist tae travel tae yer Auntie's. So, yer dyin' ma gie'd me your fare tae git myself on the day's carriage and I'm getting mysel oot o' here till the fever leaves oor wee Haven. Efter 'a, I dinnae want tae catch whit abody thinks you hae. Ye look sick enough tae hae the fever, 'specially cos I marked your neck wi a real lookin rash. Onyway you'll soon catch it if you stay here long enough."

I don't understand. He smiles down at me but his eyes are black and angry and he spits on me when he talks.

"Ye never knew you was livin'. I want a chance tae live an' hae my children's children enjoy a'thing you had. I'm going tae be the wan tae survive the fever, no Wattie. I'll gie his Auntie yer love, will I?"

I can't see him. My eyes won't seem to stay open.

"Fareweel, Jason. It took a while, but dead folks hae great patience, as you'll find oot fer yersel soon enough."

At last, Dead Ed's called me by my name. Just like proper best pals.

SMALL SACRIFICES

Beth Blackmore

"You started it!" cried Mary, pale and breathless from the scuffle. "But eh'm gonna feenish it, Billy Cathcart, for eh'm havin a word wi your Da the night." She squeeshed down on the skinny lad squirming under the weight of her heavy boot and forced his face into a dollop of muck that was sticking to the factory floor. A shiver ran down her back as she felt for the first time in her life the thrill of being a winner.

"Mary! Mary! Mary!" the mill lassies chorused.

Mary's blunted fingertips swiped at the loose strands of hair sticking about her face. The open wound on her blue-bruised elbow was too sore to touch but somehow less painful to bear than the long rip reaching down the sleeve of her blouse.

"From here on keep that wee gropin hand tae yersel, Billy Cathcart, an keep this bloody flair clean an aw!" She spat out a thread of raw jute. "When meh Da gets his job back he'll mak sure ye sweep it as clean as a new peen!"

At the mention of her father and his wretched situation she felt the fire in her belly begin to fizzle out. Billy was lying motionless and completely silent.

"Git up, ye daft wee sod," she whispered, holding out

her hand, but he scrambled out of reach and hauled himself to his feet, his watery gaze settling sullenly on her shining eyes. He drew his snotty nose across his sleeve as he limped away, his body distorted by the flickering of the yellow light filtering down from the high ceiling.

He started it, Mary assured herself as she picked up her shawl, always hankering to be one of the lively lads when all he was fit for was pushing the stoor brush around the mill floor. Even the army didn't want him or any of the wee bauchles that worked at 'the low mill'. Funny to think of it as a blessing that her wee brother Willie could not even manage a morning's work here, not since he was made a cripple years ago when a big lassie came galloping down the plettie stairs and knocked him backwards all the way to the bottom.

Her thoughts were interrupted by a voice softly calling her name. It was the guid-looking Samuel Paterson who took the fancy of most of the mill women. Her cheeks warmed.

"Weel done, bonnie Mary," he cooed. She smiled at him hoping she looked to his liking. "Gonnae fight *me* noo cos the lads here aboot want tae see yer braa bare legs agin, high-kicking it oot frae under that fine lace petticoat." Mary turned on her heel and walked quickly away from him. It wasn't a lace petticoat as he well knew. It was her only petticoat, patterned into holes by a determined rat.

Eyes smarting, Mary ignored the group of excited lads dancing behind her. Instead, she linked arms with the women to help shepherd the reluctant children to the looms, some of whom were clowning the recent skirmish, while others, darting hasty looks at Mary, wiped their eyes as if in relief to have the disturbance over. She watched as they now crawled like little beetles between the machines that left dumps of oily fibres to be picked clean by short stumpy fingers.

The spontaneous bantering of the sisterhood of spinners did nothing to change her darkening mood for she knew that even if another bairn cried or pee'd herself or fell into a dead-shaped body desperate for sleep, only to be smacked into wakefulness, she was powerless to change such brutal treatment. Yesterday she had tried to stop wee John McIvor thumping at his forehead with his knuckle-white fist, shivering in clothes sodden with cold pee one minute then shivering in a flush of hot sweat the next. No-one had seen him today.

Mary was jolted out of her dark reverie as Maister Tamson's pugnacious voice reverberated around the mill, causing her to jump, more in fright than in fear.

"If there's been ony fightin, then you're aa oot!"

Tamson's face was as crumpled and stained as her purple skirt as he bore down on her and she reeled at the whiffy smell of the drink being breathed into her face.

'Eh'm oot o' meh office for twa minutes an ye lot start fightin. Wha started it this time?" he bawled, looking straight at Mary. "It wis yersel, eh?" he said with a growl and a finger to her face that reminded Mary of the way he was accustomed to addressing his mangy dog. Before she could deny it, he jerked his thumb in the direction of the office.

Mary stood in front of Tamson's big table or 'meh desk', as he liked to call it, with her back to the office window overlooking the mill floor. She kept her dark eyes riveted on the inkwell as Tamson started to rant, brandishing pens and shoving papers. His sweat reminded her of the day he had nearly collapsed with the effort of moving the selfsame table to face the window so that he could spy on his *'world of wanton wimmen'*. Well, he could aye wish!

Of course the lassies soon discovered what he was about so that when he cuff-rubbed a peerie spot on the inside of the window they would signal to each other, using the only language possible when the whole factory was trembling with the growling and clanking of the big machines being whipped into hellish music. By the time his beery eye appeared they would have turned to the window to jiggle their bubbies, laughing hysterically as the spot misted up.

"Wipe that grin aff yer face, Mary Gartshore, or eh'll dae it for ye," cried Tamson, and she did, for, with a flourish, he had dipped a pen into the inkwell, bent over the big black book and put a cross against her name. God, he might dock some pay this time. Another one and she would be given her books for there were plenty queuing up to take her place at the spinning Jenny.

The days had begun to shorten noticeably and, as the evening light strained to peer in through the kitchen window, it sought to make patterns on the faces of Mary and her younger brother as they sat huddled together on the rag rug rumpled on the floor. Mary pushed her brother away from her and frowned.

"Aggie's no washed yer face," she said, spitting on her hand.

"Dinna even think o' it," said Willie, burrowing into her shawl.

She pulled his useless legs into the folds of her skirt then stretched the shawl around them both, muffling their hands together. Soon their Da would come in with a hearty song on his lips and nothing in his pockets and, if he didn't fall over, fumble about the banked up fire. And kind Aggie, the only person she'd ever trust to look after her wee brother, had once again brought some bone broth with her when she'd carried Willie home.

Then the banging started. "Present for ye Mary," cried a sing -song voice from the plettie landing. "Fae ye know who. A wee reminder tae watch yer step. Us men dinnae tak kindly tae lassies gettin cocky, that's oor job."

The door jamb was being hauled off amid hollers and squeals until they were stomped out by the sound of boots leaping down the stairs. Mary held up a hush finger at Willie for 'roarin fou' drunks careering about the plettie stairs were not to be confronted. The scurrilous voices died away.

Inching the front door open, Mary reeled from the stench rising from the papers at her feet, smeared with black shite. She gathered them up and backed into the lobby, kicking the door shut. Willie began dragging himself towards her.

"Aw Mary, whit've ye done?"

She stuffed the festering bundle into the piss bucket then dropped down beside him. "Eh know who's responsible Willie an eh'm gonna dae somethin aboot it. Climb on." Willie locked his arms around her neck, legs dangling like a disjointed dolly, as she tottered down the staircase towards Billy Cathcart's door and a word with his Da.

"Ye smell o' shite, Mary," whispered Willie as Jock Cathcart opened the door hiccoughing and scratching.

The high walls of the buildings dulled the piercing screeches of some 'singing canaries', seemingly unaffected by the bone-cold night as they engaged in some lively and noisy festivities. As Mary picked her way through the drunken lassies, a figure hung out perilously far from a high window tugging at the washing stretching out on the line strung between the buildings. A shrill utterance from a baby interrupted her thoughts and sent her quick-stepping over the greasy cobbles towards the meeting house.

Her father had talked his usual nonsense when he came home from the pub, bewailing their misfortunes and blaming himself, which was stupid. She had corralled him at home with the promise she knew she couldn't keep of a little money to spend when she returned but his downy hair and translucent grey skin pulling tightly across the bones of his cheeks hinted at something else sucking the life out of him.

More often than not she found that the world inside her head was no better than the world outside. So much had changed over the last five years. Mammy gone, Da paid off, Willie's accident. She'd even lost the scent of hot, strong tea and soft new bread, and a dab of rosewater. Although there were only the three of them now her mill wages were not enough, and sharing impossible dreams with Willie made her heart ache. She would have all the life wrung out of her if things went on as they were.

The smoky pockets of gloom spooked her as she picked her way over the ground, rank with today's filth and yesterday's glaur. When a heap of dirty sacking shifted, and something buried beneath it snorted, she ran head down round the corner mumbling, 'Oor faither which art in heaven…..' and into the sharp teeth of a winter's night.

The street's icy breath caught her by the throat and made her cough. She stopped, unprepared for the sight of the ill-dressed children clustered outside the church hall, some waving at her with faces raked red and white by the clawing cold; others standing in shivering huddles, their string-thin necks laid bare.

A cup slipped from a small chapped hand missing two fingers. Then suddenly, the hall door rattled noisily and scraped open to reveal a hearty tambourine being bashed by an elderly lady who quickly disappeared amidst the steaming breaths from argumentative children jostling their way inside, their battered cups held up in high hopes of a sweet drink. Mary ran into the nearby close, up the spiralling stair and through a door on the second landing.

Inside the kitchen, six young women had doubled up on three of the four chairs.

"Sorry eh'm late," panted Mary and sat beside Aggie.

"Remember, walls have ears, so keep yer voices down," Betty mouthed. Aggie raised her finger for a word. The room quietened.

"We've had umpteen hecklins and walkoots this year for equal pay wi the few men folk left, an it's no made ony difference. They're useless, fur we jist git another lockoot."

"Aye, but it made a difference when we rubbed thick black treacle ower John Simpson's windae for putting up the price o' his bread every week," said Ena. "Mind ye, yon crowd o' bairns had it licked aff in nae time."

The question of Tam McLeod's recent sacking caused much discussion about the cruel selfishness of the employers but Mary's head still ran with the pictures of the small suffering children she witnessed every day.

"We've no made a stooshie yet aboot the wee pickers and shifters havin tae work such lang hours when they're still ower young," she pleaded.

"We agreed aboot the order o things, Mary," said Betty. "Equal pay first, hoosing second, then the bairns. We'll no forget the bairns."

"Eh'll look efter any bairn that needs me," said Carrie. "For meh hairt bleeds when a man becomes the kettle-biler in his ane hoose, but ye'll no guess whit's happening noo." She stood up to impart her latest bit of knowledge. "Eh've heard that some o' Tam McLeod's wee bairns kin be pickers if he pays Doctor Broon 3d, for he'll write oot a paper saying they're aw nine an well enough tae work."

Ena wished a bucket of horse shite on the doctor's head!

Another disturbance for equal pay was arranged by the outraged women for two days hence.

"Yer quiet the night, Mary," whispered Aggie.

"The tap ootside oor closie is frozen an naebody has water." Mary's voice cracked. "An eh've jist passed a thrang o' cauld bairns needin a guid feed. Where's the justice o' it aa'?" The words tumbled out of her so quickly that nobody had time to answer.

Aggie pulled Mary to her feet. "Ye're ower tired," she said. "It's time tae head fur hame." The others nodded their agreement.

"At sometime we'll need tae dae something.... spectacular," said Ena, "so thae mill owners'll sit up an tak notice."

"Aye, an if it's really spectacular it'll bring the newspaper man tae Lochee, see if it dinna," Betty McAndrew promised.

The ground glistened under the sluggish rain as Mary and Aggie approached the church hall where the children's singing was getting higher and higher until it burst into peals and squeals of laughter. "Maybe there are some fates that can be changed," whispered Mary.

"It's Daisy McHoul runs this branch o' the Total Abstinence Society," said Aggie, searching Mary's face.

"The bairns'll be telt tae get their mammies and da's tae sign the pledge card agreeing no tae touch a drop o' the hard stuff, unless they're nae weel. She'll tell them that the evil drink swallows doon aa oor money and that's why we wear ragged claes an end up deid, but eh dinna accept we're aa bound for hell, cos we already bide in it." She laughed. "For half an hour they've stepped oot o' hell the night and intae a bairn's paradise where they can hae fun and sing and get a sweet drink."

Aggie sat down heavily on the cold step, nodding her head thoughtfully. "People like us think we canna change things, but we can. Aye, even jist one o' us can mak a difference. It's a bit like sacrificing yersel for something ye think mair important, mair worthy. Aye, worthwhile is hard-won, Mary." She rubbed her backside. "Meh bum's freezing, so let's gang hame."

Mary's mouth stretched into a smile as she hauled Aggie up.

Willie wagged a serious finger at his sister as they sat on the rug. "Aw Mary, eh'm gettin terrible thoughts that yer up tae something."

Mary's bright eyes held his. "Eh want tae mak a difference for the bairns, Willie. Gettin het up and shoutin dinna. It needs tae be somethin spectacular. Eh've talked it ower wi' Aggie an she'll look efter ye if eh'm held up the morrow." She plucked at her ravelling skirt.

Willie looked up at the window. "Look Mary, it's

Mammy's star."

She cradled his body close to hers and, as if entranced by the twinkling sparkle, their tired eyes closed.

The final grasp of darkness lifted from the deep corners of the kitchen as Mary prepared to go to work. All will be well, she assured herself, looking down on her sleeping brother, for Aggie would be here to look after him and her Da when she was gone. As she stood on the brink of leaving, Mary's outstretched hand hovered towards Willie's frizzy head causing the palpitations in her breast to grow stronger. Then her hand fell to quietly closing the door between them.

Her heart now pounding like a drum, Mary strode towards the mill. Some of the children caught up with her and held tightly to her hands and skirt so that together they walked smartly towards the mill door, its wailing bummer warning them to be on time, or else.

Soon the steam engines were turning the spinning frames and drawing the fibres to the exact thickness. Mary checked the fibres twisting themselves in readiness to bind together in a continuous thread and wind the yarn around the bobbins. She looked about her. Everyone was busy. No-one was looking her way, so no-one was alarmed by the wild waves of rebellion behind her tranced eyes until she flung her head back and let out a long high howl as she yanked at her ill-fitting skirt, dropping it quickly to her ankles. Picking it up, she waved it high above her head and then hurled it at her Jenny. The skirt caught between the teeth of the machine which growled then stuttered to an ailing halt. Everything was ripped to shreds. Mary felt sick and sicker still when she heard Tamson's voice.

"Mother o' God, Mary Gartshore's gone ravin mad. Steer clear o' her," he was yelling. "Christ, the Jenny's no workin. Whit's the boss gonna dae tae us?" Mary's closed eyes could well imagine his purple-splodged face and trembling body as his words poured out in one continuous and impassioned stream.

She could even understand why the young men cursed her and why some bairns cried and some laughed.

"Run and get the newspaper man," cried Ena.

"Naw, send for the polis," bawled Tamson.

Mary slumped to her knees, exhausted. She gave up her few ineffectual struggles as Samuel lifted her up into his arms, his soft voice blowing lightly over her face.

"Stupid, aye, bonnie Mary, but brave, ower brave."

MRS DARGIE'S REVENGE

Jean Langlands

Jeannie Miller gazed out of the farmhouse kitchen window at the rolling landscape and the sea beyond. Swirls of grey mist were creeping over the fields, sometimes obscuring the figures working there, sometimes revealing them. There was indecision in the air; a cold crispness that might turn to ice, or melt into rain. Behind her she could hear Maggie, the other housemaid, clattering about with the pots and pans. Then suddenly the noise stopped.

"Do ye know what people are sayin'? They're sayin' Annie Nicoll's expecting a bairn."

"She's no!"

"Aye, an' ah ken wha the faither is."

Jeannie Miller dropped the potato she was peeling into the bucket of icy water and wiped her hands on her apron. "Oh, my god Maggie, wha is it?"

"They're sayin' it's the farmer himsel."

"No Mr. Dargie?"

"Aye. Dae ye no mind at the Hairst they were aye gaein' aff thegither? Folk were speakin' aboot it then. And Mrs. Dargie was away up tae Glen Isla tae see her sister."

"She'll be mad aboot this if she finds oot."

"Oh, she's heard a' right and she's no pleased aboot it. Nothing goes past her, an her man's always had an eye for the women."

Maggie Stewart sat down on the wooden kitchen chair and smoothed down her long black skirt. Jeannie could see she was pleased to have imparted this piece of information and was no doubt rejoicing at the thought of all the others still to be told. Jeannie scooped up the peeled potatoes and flung them into the pot of water that was spitting on the open fire. She picked up the brass poker and, deep in thought, began to rearrange the logs in the grate. "She's said nothin' to me. I canna believe it o' Annie. She's aye been the quiet ane."

"Oh, but they're the ones to watch, Jeannie. There's goin' to be trouble, you mark my words."

The back door opened and young Davie Donaldson appeared.

"And speakin' o' trouble. Get oot o' here wi yer mucky shoon."

"I'm no mucky. It's honest work I'm da'en, liftin the neeps."

"Awa wi ye, you've never been honest in yer life."

Maggie grabbed a potato and threw it at him, but he caught it in his hand and fielded it back to her.

"Mr. Dargie says ane o' ye is tae meet his wife aff the carriage at the road end." He grinned and winked at Maggie.

She glared back at him. "I'm no goin'. She'll be in a right bad mood."

"How's that?"

"Have ye no heard aboot Annie Nicoll and Mr. Dargie?" Davie's face darkened but he said nothing and went quickly back outside.

It was a long walk to the end of the farm track and a long wait when she got there. Jeannie was glad of the company of Bess, the farm collie, who had followed her, unconcerned about the dreich November weather and the mud underfoot. There was no sign of the carriage and it was getting dark. Could it be true what Maggie had told her? She might be a bit of a gossip, but usually she was right.

Poor Annie, she must have been too ashamed to confide in anyone, not even herself, who'd always taken a kindly interest in her. After all, she had worked here for three years, before Annie and Maggie came on the scene. She'd always done her best to help them. It was her Christian duty, she felt, but she was real fond of them both. Then there was Davie, who'd always had a fancy for Annie. He'd gone real quiet when he heard the news.

"Lie doon, Bess, that's right, lie on ma feet and warm them up. I'm frozen."

She could hardly see for the fog now and was

taken aback when she heard the sound of feet approaching. Bess began to bark then wagged her tail. It was Davie and he was out of breath.

"I'm sorry for givin' you a fright. I've got to speak to you. It's no true what they're sayin' about Annie."

"How do ye mean? Is she no havin' a bairn?" Jeannie felt relief begin to flood over her.

"Aye, she is, and it's mine, but we haven't told anyone yet."

Jeannie wondered what the minister would have to say but she bit her tongue.

It was as if he had read her thoughts.

"It's aricht, we're goin' tae get married, and I could murder that Maggie Stewart for spreadin' this gossip. I don't want my Annie to hear aboot this."

Jeannie reassured him she would say nothing.

"Ye see, she was asked by the farmer to make his wife a shawl for her Christmas. It was to be a surprise. You know Annie's affa guid at the knittin' and she had tae go an' get the wool, and Mr. Dargie paid for it. That's why they were talking in secret."

"Aye, right enough, I mind o' that."

"But folk have got the wrong idea."

"It's terrible how these rumours can start, Davie. It's a real mess and it's no something you could talk aboot tae the Dargies."

"No, I dinna ken what to do. I'd best get back."

It was some time before the carriage light appeared in the distance, bobbing in and out of sight. She could hear the rattle of the wheels and the chink of the bridles and bits. Minutes later the horses were there beside her, snorting with the effort of the long climb up the hill, their hot steamy breath visible in the air. She could smell the leather harness and the heat from their bodies.

"Ye're late Jim, what kept ye?"

"Oh, we'd no ten minutes left Pitkerro when the grey mare went lame. She'd lost a shoe. Young Wullie here had tae mind the carriage while I walked up tae Bucklershead for anither horse."

While they were speaking Wullie had jumped down to open the carriage doors.

Jeannie greeted her employer. "Evenin', Mrs. Dargie, will I take your bags?"

"Aye lass, there's plenty here to carry. No, no, I'll carry this parcel myself. Come on Bess, stop your barkin'."

"Have you got the dinner on for Mr. Dargie and the men? They'll be starvin' after pullin' neeps aa day."

"Aye, Maggie's seein' tae it. Did ye have a nice day in Dundee Mrs. Dargie?"

"Aye I did, I've got everything I needed. But it was a long wait doon at Kellas for anither horse." She lapsed into silence, and Jeannie knew better than to speak further. They tramped on up the farm track, each deep in her own thoughts. For a time the fog seemed to envelop them.

It was as they neared the farmhouse door that Mrs. Dargie tripped and dropped her parcel. Jeannie bent down to pick it up.

"Give it here, don't you touch that." An impatient hand snatched it back, but not before Jeannie had caught a glimpse of the label through the sodden brown paper. Suddenly the chill of the night air seemed to seep into her bones.

An appetising smell of stew filled the air as they opened the kitchen door. Maggie had set the long wooden table and was mashing the potatoes. The men would soon be in from the fields, and Annie too, for she'd always worked outside along with some of the other lassies. She seemed to enjoy it, for she was strong and robust. Jeannie often envied her friend the outdoor life, especially in the summertime, when she herself was stuck indoors cleaning the big house with Maggie, and Mrs. Dargie always watching them.

Dinner was a friendly affair, with plenty of talk of the day's work and jokes among the men. Annie Nicoll looked well enough, but she kept her head down and said little. That was aye Annie's way, thought Jeannie. She still couldn't believe the news about her and Davie. She wondered if she herself would ever get married. No one had ever taken an interest in her, and here she was nearly twenty-one already. She sighed.

Mr. Dargie had always been good to his workers and Friday night was a bit special. After the meal the men began to smoke, then Davie Donaldson got out his fiddle and began to rosin the bow.

"Come on Davie, gie us a tune."

"Aye well, wait till ah've tuned up."

"Hurry up then, gie us a Neil Gow tune."

"Right then, here we go."

A few long chords with his bow, then he was off.

There was some tappin' of feet and humming of the tunes. Maggie Stewart grabbed a partner and got up to dance. She was always the bold one, thought Jeannie. Never a care in the world. Mrs. Dargie, on the other hand, looked surly, and her husband had gone off with some friends to talk business in the other room. Jeannie felt uneasy, though she couldn't say why. She would have to try and talk to Annie tonight and warn her to be careful of Mrs. Dargie, for that woman was in an ill humour.

After a while someone called over to Annie. "C'mon, gie's a sang, lass. Ye're fair quiet the nicht."

"Aye, c'mon Annie, let's here that lovely voice of yours."

Davie put down the fiddle and watched her intently as she began to sing. After a while she returned his gaze and smiled as she sang.

Oh the broom, the bonnie bonnie broom
The broom o' the Cowdenknowes
Fain would I be in my ain country
Herdin' ma faithers ewes.

As she finished Davie winked at her. "That was great, Annie." He picked up the fiddle again and began to play a slow air, a sad lilting tune. Jeannie watched them. She hoped they would get married soon and put an end to all this gossip. She crossed the room and sat down beside Annie.

"I've got tae talk to ye," she whispered. "C'mon outside for a minute."

"Och, it's too cauld outside an' it's that foggy. It's creepy."

"It's important."

"Is it about me an' Davie? Ye've heard, haven't you?"

"Aye, I've heard some rumours."

They were interrupted by Maggie. "What are you two whispering about?"

"Och, none of your business."

"Well, it must be interesting cos you're both red in the face."

Jeannie resigned herself to the waiting game, and sat back to enjoy the music.

By ten thirty folk were getting tired, and the men started to make tracks for the bothy while the women tidied up the kitchen. After a while Mrs Dargie emerged from the pantry, carrying a tray of drinks.

"She's got a face like soor milk," Maggie was heard to whisper.

"Here ye are lassies. Thanks for all your help tonight." She placed the tray on the wooden table beside Annie.

"Now here's a drink for each of you. I've made them masel', wi' some nice herbs and spices. Aye, ye'll sleep weel the nicht."

She handed each of the girls a drink, turning to Annie last with a smile on her face which did not reach her eyes but the door opened suddenly and Mr. Dargie appeared. With a grin he took the drink from his wife's hand and downed it in one. "Thanks, love," he said.

It was a few days later that Mr. Dargie died of the cholera. That's what the doctor said anyway. He was buried in the little churchyard near to the farm, and the minister spoke eloquently about the mysterious ways of the Lord while the mourners shivered in the icy wind that had blown away the last of the mist and fog. Only Jeannie knew that the poor dead man had taken the poisoned drink meant for Annie. Hadn't she seen the label with her own eyes when Mrs. Dargie dropped her parcel?

And it said quite plainly on the little box, 'Arsenic'.

THE COFFIN ROAD

David Carson

"Haud fast tae the stave. Walk slowly and mind waur ye pit your feet. Keep in step."

The words of caution echoed through my head. I was breathing heavily, unevenly. How can I keep this up? I wondered with growing panic. Five miles over rough ground, and steep in places. I was beginning to gasp for breath. Why was I doing this? I looked at the others. They walked with shoulders erect, not a bead of sweat, not a foot out of step. The stave dug into my hand, but I couldn't change position. Where was the next cairn - a mile away at least. No rest until then. I don't think I can manage.

Suddenly my brogue slid on an icy rock. I stumbled forward, letting go of the stave. I grabbed wildly, knocking the bearer in front of me out of his stride. As I fell to the ground I saw, as if in slow motion, the black feathers flutter incongruously in the air, and land softly, four smudges in the snow. The coffin slid from the staves and crashed, corner-first, into the hard ground. I watched, aghast, as the casket split from the lid, then turned over, ejecting the body within into the midst of the flailing group.

"Patrick, Patrick, wake up man! Whit's wrang? Ye're

thrashing like a scytheman!"

The horrifying images slowly dissolved, to be replaced by Jamie's face moving above my own.

I sat up. "A dream, Jamie," I muttered in relief. "Nothing but a dream - vivid but ephemeral, and of no lasting harm."

Jamie did not look convinced. He pushed his hand though his hair, still thick but prematurely grey - and gave me a hard look. His face was more lined than I remembered, but his eyes retained their sharp intelligence.

"Dinna scorp, Patrick. Abody can hear you've been awa' for a wheen o' years. Ye can be gabbie wi your freens frae the south country, but mind whaur ye are noo. I just want tae mak certain sure you're fine after your journey - and for what lies ahead. Anyway," he continued, "I ken why you're agitated. It's your brither. It's Rab, isn't it?"

I nodded.

"He wis a fine man. That it should come to this…" The sadness in his voice lingered in the silence. But I detected reproach as well.

"Go on, Jamie, say it. Rab stayed, I left. He worked the farm, I went off to do different things, and I abandoned my responsibilities."

Jamie's expression hardened. "I dinna like it when you go putting yir ain thoughts intae my mouth. That being said, mind, I never really jaloused why you left, Patrick. There was a puckle chat at the time, but I didna gie it heed. I mind Brigitte seemed ower fashed, but she spak little, at least tae me."

95

Jamie paused. He was clearly waiting for me to say something, provide an explanation. But I wasn't ready for that. I turned the conversation to more pressing issues.

"Jamie, tell me again what you ken o' Rab's death."

He frowned. "His body was found at the fit o' the cliffs north-east o' the Monega Hill in Caenlochan Glen. The first sign o' ill was when his horse was seen at Auchavan in Glen Isla, wi' nae sign o' Rab."

I was taken aback. "But that's all of twenty miles frae here. What on earth was he doing o'er there?"

Jamie shrugged. "I dinna richt ken. He'd gang off on his own on lang rides quite often - mair an' mair in fact."

"But what about the farm?" I said. I had been surprised, on my arrival the previous evening, at how unkempt the farm looked. I had had to shoo hens out of the kitchen - there was even a nest in the corner - and the front door hung askew. There was a general air of neglect.

Jamie hesitated. "At first he used to say he was awa' tae check the sheep - some o' his ewes ended up backit on account o' their lang wool, and he'd lost his orraman tae anither farm. In fact he lost a lot o' sheep as well." Then he added, as if to himself, "Aye, Rab, you were losing so much."

I let that hang in the air for a few moments, and Jamie went on, "The doctor said he died from the injuries tae his heid, from the fall off his horse an' doon the cliffs."

Images from my dream flashed through my head. "Jamie, Rab was a guid horseman."

"Aye, that's true. It's richt strange."

I waited. Jamie shifted uncomfortably from one foot to the other. "I'm sweir tae say mair. Ithers'll nae be sae quiet."

"Meaning what, Jamie?"

There was silence.

"Can you at least tell me what Brigitte has to say aboot a' this?"

"She can speak for hersel."

I could see I would get nothing more from Jamie. It was time to move on.

When I had received word of my brother Rab's death three days before, my reactions were equivocal. I was surprised - the younger brother shouldn't predecease the elder - then I felt guilt that surprise and not grief was uppermost. But five years had distanced me from glen life in general. I had moved on. I had studied, gained work in the employ of a respected lawyer - only as a clerk, but I had ambitions. I had settled in Glasgow. I was only 35, life was before me, rich in opportunity and pleasure. Glasgow in 1885 was vibrant, energetic, optimistic.

These and similar thoughts preoccupied me as I walked up towards Brigitte's cottage. On impulse I turned off the track and took the path up Glen Tairie. It was a cold and clear morning. Patches of snow lingered in shaded crannies, and the pure air was like a tonic. I had almost forgotten how invigorating it could be to walk the glen in early morning. I left the path and clambered to the top of Knachly hill. I realised suddenly that I was retracing steps that Rab and I had frequently taken as boys; I, the protective elder brother, he the young enthusiast, eager to see, try, learn everything.

Words our mother used to say to us when we returned from such days came back to me. She said it was a poem she'd learned, and she'd changed it for us, something like:

Brithers baith, ye clamb the hill thegither,

and mony a canty day ye've had wi' ane anither.

Ahead, the Clova mountains reared into place. I slowed as my gaze followed the ridges, slung like slackened tight-ropes between the tops. Familiar outcrops glinted in the aftermath of a shower, and grass glistened clear of the shadows of an intermittent sun. I felt a sudden tightness in my throat and dampness in my eyes as I succumbed to a flash flood of memories. Rab ate his first averins above Kilbo, enjoying how thirst-quenching they were. Sometimes we spent hours picking them, eating them, crushing them and painting our faces and arms in their juice. Aye Rab, that's when I startit tae call ye Cam Ruadh, and ye were richt pleased until the dominie learnt ye the history o' the ugliest, fiercest pockmarked wee man o' the glens! I mind the day I dared ye tae eat hare droppings - I tellt ye they were special mountain eggs, and ye believed me! Oh, the look on your face when ye bit intae it.

I raised my gaze again to the surrounding hills, and stared. Suddenly I felt frustration, impotence. How can you be so solid, so imposing, yet so indifferent, I almost shouted at them. I shook myself fiercely to get rid of these memories, like an animal shaking surface water from its coat. I flung a last, almost defiant look around me, and hurried downwards to the valley floor.

I approached Brigitte's cottage with an unquiet mind. I had not seen her since that day five years ago when I told her I was leaving the glen. I remember she had been calm. But she made one remark that stayed in my mind.

"Your heart's desire is there for the taking Patrick, if only ye could recognise it."

I opened the gate and went into the garden. It looked tended, alive, even on this February day. Kale grew in a large bed, and elsewhere the remains of nettles, wild thyme and other herbs were visible. I suddenly had a picture of Rab pulling bog-myrtle stems and smelling their fragrant resin. I looked away sharply. Flower pots - an unusual adornment in glen gardens - were grouped beneath the kitchen window. The door of the lean-to byre was open, and I could see stores of wood piled neatly. Smoke rose straight from the chimney into the still air, and I breathed deeply, momentarily enveloped in the peaty atmosphere so evocative of the glen. I knocked gently on the door, and then more loudly. Silence. I pushed it open, and entered.

I went into the kitchen, and looked round. Crockery sat in neatly-washed order next to the sink. She can't be far, I thought, and as if in confirmation I heard footsteps lightly striking the stone floor of the hall.

"Patrick," said Brigitte, "I thocht I spied you earlier, coming off the hill." She spoke as if to confirm a daily occurrence, with no hint of surprise or apprehension. "I heard you were back," she continued, then paused. "Sad times."

I looked at her, and she returned my gaze, eyes clear and frank. Her long auburn hair was parted in the centre and fell half-way down her back. The pale sheen of her skin contrasted with the dark wool of her dress which flowed from her neck to her ankles in a sweeping line broken only by the swell of her breasts. "Bonnie Brigitte wi' the braw bosom." My adolescent fantasy leapt unbidden into my mind and I felt my face colour.

"Sad indeed," I said, and added hurriedly, "I arrived yestreen. I went to the farm, and Jamie kept me company."

"He's a guid man, and a faithful friend."

"Aye. You look well. The years haven't aged you."

"Thank you. I wish I could say that life goes on, yet, as we ken, Patrick, that is not always the case."

I was not sure if she was inviting me to speak about us, or about Rab, but I let the moment pass.

"Do you want to sit?" she asked. "We can move to the parlour."

I followed her and we took seats opposite each other.

"You seem to manage," I said, gesturing round the well-furnished room.

"Aye. I help oot the governess wi' the laird's bairns - and ye ken that my parents left me well provided for. I often think it is a pity neither lived long after their move here."

"And what of Rab? Did you think o' him with pity?"

100

"You still twist things, don't you Patrick? I hoped your years away micht hae helped you to see ithers in a better light."

"I'm sorry, Brigitte. I'm sometimes clumsy in what I say. What I meant… I wondered…"

"You want to know how things stood between Rab and me?"

"Yes."

"He's dead, Patrick." Her tone was brusque, harsh even.

"But you know him, knew him, better than anyone. You lived with him, for a while at any rate, you must hae some notion."

"I can see that you have not been entirely cut off from life up here these five years."

"But I know very little!" I continued as calmly as I could. "I've seen the farm - it's a mess."

Brigitte was staring at the fire. "It didna happen all of a sudden," she said eventually. "It was mair one thing on top o' anither."

"You used to say that Rab could cope wi' just about anything. He seemed tae have all the qualities you admired."

"Aye. But things changed after you left".

"What do you mean?"

Brigitte thought for a moment. "I think it had to do with taking responsibility. Up till then he always had you, even if you didna dae much to help oot."

"Come Brigitte. He knew that I had nae real interest in farming, that I wouldn't be around forever."

"And you knew how he felt aboot a' that?"

"No. But I'm sure you did!" The words came out almost in spite, but Brigitte didn't rise to my tone.

"It's true I spent time with him. He was a very steadfast person".

"You always preferred his company to mine." Something cold appeared in Brigitte's expression. "That's very hurtful, Patrick. But that should no' surprise me. I learned a long time ago that your world has little space for anybody save yourself."

I wanted to protest, but Brigitte continued, "Have you forgotten the times we spent thegither, Patrick? Those were more intimate than anything that passed between Rab and me." She paused and stared intently at me. "Why, Patrick, are you blushing? Are you ashamed of what we did together? Have you forgotten how, afterwards, we lay close, and you would tell me o' a' your plans, your ambitions? Perhaps if I had listened mair closely then I would ha' seen that there was nae place for me in that ideal world o' yours."

"Brigitte, did ye really think…"

"Aye," she interrupted, "why otherwise would I hae found myself in the state I was after you left."

"State? What sort o' state?"

Brigitte stared at the floor, as if she had said too much, but her silence was more eloquent than words.

"Brigitte, were you…?"

"Wi' child? Aye. And I felt mair alane than I have ever felt since. And so I went to Rab and told him. He said I was tae come and bide with him, that he would say the baby was his. I knew he wanted to care for me."

Tears welled in her eyes.

"I did go to Rab's, that bit you heard was true. But…"

"But what, Brigitte?"

"I fell ill after three months and lost the baby."

I got up and moved towards her, but she pushed me away.

"No Patrick, no gestures, no fine words. I want nothing from you."

I flinched. I thought to have lost a brither. Now I had lost a son as well. She went on, "I felt estranged from the world through my loss. Rab wanted to continue as we were, as if nothing had happened. I could not. I know he felt rejected, but I could not help myself. That moment marked the beginning of his unhappiness, of the restless state he could not escape."

I felt faint. "Brigitte, you must tell me what happened. If ye dinna, I will find Jamie and get the truth frae him."

"I wish I could believe that your concern does you credit, Patrick, but perhaps it is your conscience that has at last found a voice."

I ignored this, and she went on.

"Rab started to disappear mair an' mair often, going off on his horse for a whole day or more. I speired an' speired, and finally he told me he had built a still in one of the corries far up Glen Isla. He was making whisky and selling it illegally. Then he began to drink it himself, and soon he had little time for onything else. Rab must have kennt it was only a matter of time afore the gaugers caught up wi' him, and what it could mean."

The thought that my brother may have killed himself filled me with desolation. I knew that Brigitte would never say, nor would anyone. Brigitte slumped back in her chair. I stood up and stared out of the window. The hills were bathed in the light of the afternoon sun - cold, implacable, eternal.

I galloped hard up the glen. I needed to see the spot where Rab had died. Monega Hill rose sharp and clean above Tulchan. I was drawn deeper and deeper into the glen, and rode on, past the cairn by the river and up to the shieling. I gazed into Caenlochan, and raised my eyes to the cliffs above. I imagined Rab's body falling into the jumble of rocks and stones.

"Rab, Rab, ye've been sic a fool - and so have I." I sat trembling in the saddle until my voice echoed into silence and my body stopped shaking. I rode back to Prosen, filled with a calm resolve.

We followed the coffin road from high in the glen down to the cemetery. Eight of us walked together, solemnly, in step, as we carried Rab to his final resting place. We stopped but once, at the coffin bridge over the river, lowering the staves slowly and carefully. When we set off again, some of Rab's friends who lined the route came forward and placed stones on the cairn beside the bridge.

The sun shone low in the east, not warm, yet casting a brightness that told of the coming spring. I felt, as we threw our handfuls of earth into the lair, that something in me was passing away as well. Yet at the same time I was filled with an anticipation about the future - anxious, but also keen and determined. My return to the glen had taught me much, not least that one's memory can be both defective and deceitful. I had forgotten how imperious yet enfolding the glen can be, and how solid and honest its people. The things that made me leave five years ago now drew me back. I had thought to find direction and purpose in the city, but now I realised I might have been wrong.

I was no farmer, of that I was sure. But times are changing here in the glen as elsewhere, and I felt certain there would be a role for me, as a bookkeeper to the estate, perhaps, or even, in due time, as dominie in the school.

I grieve for Rab and what his life became, but when I ponder on that I see my own road, only now I hope to follow it back to a rebirth and a new beginning.

THE BALLAD O' THE CHIEFTAIN

Lesley Holmes

The Chieftain sailed in the year '84
Northward from Dundee,
To seek out whale in the vast Arctic chill -
Captain, John Gellatly.

They sailed in spring, for the deep frozen mass,
Aboard for Baffin Bay!
Deprivation, danger, death would they face,
Eager for prize and pay.

In Greenland they dallied in search of prey,
When the lookout shouted 'Fall!'
Crews raced to their stations - set for the fight,
Woe to latecomers all.

Then whale boats four were dropped into the brine,
Five men each in pursuit,
Crews paddled their oars - in silence, of course
So as not to scare their loot.

For twenty four hours crews hunted their kill,
Exhausted by the chase,
Fired harpoons - twin-barbed - abaft the whales' fins,
And fastened boats to fish.

The whales they dived deep to escape their fate,
'til blow-holes spouted blood,
The headsmen speared with slender iron lance,
Until the whales were dead.

Then a ghostly shroud fell o'er those brave men,
A fog both dense and cold,
They cut themselves free from their hard won prize,
As panic soon took hold.

The boats circled round in search of their ship,
Visible markers - nil.
Two days they drifted, exposed and frostbit,
Lost, in treacherous chill.

Gellatly led them to frozen ice pack,
Their raging thirst to slake,
With spars from the boats they lit fire for warmth,
And refuge they did make.

Then sighting a barque some miles from the shore,
They signalled with all their might.
The three masted ship failed to answer their call,
Unable to see their plight.

With food all gone and no rescue in sight,
Gellatly hoisted sail,
And with Allan, Ford, old Robertson and Smith
Steered on to Iceland, all.

A wild raging storm then parted the four,
Gellatly rowed for their lives,
Paddled for miles through hunger and cold, then
Reached Langanaes, safe!

When three days had passed, they spied yet more hope:
A schooner bound for home.
They boarded for Leith, the Twelfth day of June,
News of comrades was none.

So what fate befell those crews left behind,
Adrift in untamed swell?
Did they meet their doom in the vast ocean deep,
Beneath that Arctic hell?

The second crew pulled twelve miles to south-east,
Led by Thomas Elder,
Returned to their ship after five days exposed then
Home on the Chieftain whaler.

Though crew number three was beset on the sea,
They made land, second June,
With frostbitten feet and one sailor dead,
By Summer were safely home.

The fourth crew capsized but righted - too late!
Buchan the steerer drowned,
Harpooner Toshie took hold the long oar
To steer them to dry land.

Drifting for days, thirst quenched with the brine,
McGregor and Cairns went mad,
Christie and Bain died from hunger and cold,
'Tosh' the last whaler lad.

Left on the sea, Toshie pleaded for death,
His legs froze to the bow,
But a passing ship cut that lonely tar free,
What would become of him now?

Those strong-hearted men that returned to Dundee,
Were funded with relief,
The Captain, his crew, all brave men and true,
Handed five pounds apiece.

So what of poor Toshie, frozen 'jack tar',
Legs cut off in his prime?
Though fame would follow the rest of his days,
No fortune would he find.

The Captain's first trip on that whaling ship,
Tested Gellatly true,
But he left this fair land and journeyed due south
A new life to pursue.

And of that whaler, did it journey again
To polar fields afar?
For seven years more it would sail the wild seas,
With many a Dundee tar.

The Chieftain last sailed the year '92,
Northward from Dundee,
Abandoned, broken, it lies forsaken,
Beneath the Arctic sea.

.

BLACKHEART

Amanda Barclay

As I rounded the corner at Gilfillan Church a vicious flurry of sleety rain hit me in the face. Icy droplets skittered over my umbrella and slipped spitefully down the back of my mackintosh collar. Fighting my way towards the office, I had a fleeting impression of a person hunkered in the door way of the fruit merchants. But so great was my rush, it registered but barely.

I ran softly up the stairs. The bright brass plaque on the wooden door identified the offices of the Gem Line Steam Shipping Company. I paused, removed my coat and only then opened the door a crack. I scanned the office. Jim, the other office junior, looked up and made to speak. Urgently I motioned him to stay quiet.

"Keep it down or buggerlugs will hear!"

He shook his head at me and returned to his work. I slipped in, shutting the door gently behind me. Twenty past eight - I really was late. Suddenly footsteps could be heard clipping smartly across the lino from the back office. I scuttled into my seat and jammed the wet raincoat under the desk. Pulling some papers in front of me, I became immediately and deeply engrossed in them. The owner of the footsteps stopped in front of my desk.

"Busy Jenkins?"

Looking up, I blinked innocently back at Mr Brown's furious red face.

"Yes, sir."

He continued to regard me.

"Been in long, have you?"

I shrugged; I was for it now.

"My office if you will."

Sullenly I followed him into his office and stood staring at his immaculately tidy desk, waiting for the tirade. He sat down and settled himself in a comfortable position to lecture me. Oh yes, I was going to be here a while.

"Second time this week you've been late. What've you to say for yourself?"

"Sorry, Sir, won't happen again, Sir."

"That's what you said last week and three weeks afore that. Oh yes, your tardy timekeeping is recorded here in my book, Jenkins," he observed smugly, "along with everything else."

It was as if he had nothing better to do than carefully note every misdemeanour of mine in that book. A hundred years from now it will probably be in a museum. People will come and marvel at the wilful wayward ways of office juniors in the 1890's.

Looking out his window I could see the swaying masts of the boats in the harbour. I longed to say I'd never wanted this rotten job, cooped up in an office and nagged all day by an angry tyrant. It was a wonder I didn't take to my bed for good. All I'd ever wanted was to go to sea and see the world. There had to be more to life than Dundee, especially on a day like this. I couldn't expect a narrow minded office manager to understand what it was to like to want for a bigger world. At home when I had mentioned my hopes for a future career, Mother had taken a dose of the vapours.

"My only son, going off to sea!"

I'd tried to reason with her – "but Father was a sailor".

"Oh yes, the sea made me a widow. If you went and were lost, it would make me a…" Here she paused, searching for the correct title for the mother of a lost son. Realising there wasn't one, she opted instead for dabbing a hanky to dry eyes and patting the region of her heart with a fluttering hand. "It would break my heart." So it was settled that I would come to work here instead.

It looked like Mr Brown was winding up to a big finale. "I did your Mother a great favour taking you on. Plenty of bright young lads who would leap at the opportunity you have been given…." He drew a breath and wagged a stubby finger at me. "Punctuality is the courtesy of Kings, never forget that. Now I am quartering your wages and noting it in my book."

Finally, or so I thought, my ordeal was over but as I backed out the office his acerbic tones chimed out again. "And retrieve that raincoat from under your desk and hang it up properly, will you?"

The old so and so missed nothing. I grabbed my coat and

went to the cloakroom. As ever it was chilly, one of Mr Brown's initiatives to discourage loitering. A row of damp overcoats hung from the coat pegs and the smell of damp wool was powerful. I noticed Mr Brown's Loden hung, not directly on a peg but on a sturdy coat hanger, so the coat would not dry misshapen.

Back in the office, the atmosphere was much warmer, with its undertone of yesterday's pipes and tobacco reek. Jim whispered across, "What did he say?"

"The usual blethers - only this time he's docking my wages." Suddenly I realised which week it was too. "Christmas week and he's docking my wages! He's no heart that one or if he has, it's black."

I was startled from my reverie of self pity as a pile of papers smacked onto my desk.

"There's shipping dockets for the *Beryl* to be checked and consolidation documents for the *Opal* to get in order, then come and see me when you're finished."

The day was relentlessly busy; Mr Brown was determined that I would make up for lost time. Meanwhile, the weather deteriorated, rain beat violent tattoos on the window and the wind whistled and rattled the big corner window. It was the kind of day when it never truly gets light and despite my resentment of the job there was something oddly companionable about being inside and warm on such a day.

Our steam vessels are all named after precious stones – the *Amethyst*, *Diamond* and *Jasper*. Their trade is varied - flax runs from Riga, linseed from Antwerp. It's a cruel irony that I should be experiencing all this exotic trade and travel second hand, through the dry medium of lading bills. But I had no time to reflect, for every time I paused Mr Brown appeared smirking with more paperwork. Eventually it was time to go home.

Setting off along Dock Street I realised Mr Brown was only just ahead of me. Having no desire to walk with him, I slowed my pace. As he passed the warehouse, a tattered looking soul emerged from the doorway and accosted him in a faltering voice. "Spare a few coppers for an old sailor?"

As I drew abreast of the two men, I realised with a shock that this must have been the person I'd seen sheltering in the doorway on my way in to work. He must have been out all day in this fearful weather. He'd get precious charity from Blackheart here.

Mr Brown's voice rang out. "Who did you sail with?"

"A servant with Dundee, Perth and London, twenty-five years till my health failed. I sailed under Captain Speedy."

"Captain Speedy you say?"

He looked at the man appraisingly and then called after me.

"Jenkins, I need your assistance here. Walk this fellow to the St Clements Mission round the corner and tell them Mr Brown insists, insists mind, that they attend to the needs of this man – what did you say your name was, sir?"

"Pettigrew, John Pettigrew."

He reached into his pocket and passed me a sum of

money. "I am trusting you on this so make sure you give this over to the director, to cover the costs for a warming meal and a bed for Mr Pettigrew here."

He turned back to the man. "Come on Pettigrew," he said not unkindly. "I've a great deal of sympathy for a fellow seafaring brother. It's a tough old life and no mistake and only too easy to fall on hard times."

He paused momentarily then, turning to me, carried on with his customary vigour. "Tell the director I will be following up on John Pettigrew so make sure he attends to his requirements well."

As we moved off together I was too stunned to speak. It appeared the tyrant had a heart after all. Mr Brown stopped at the tram stop as his tram rumbled into sight. As he got on he turned. "And be on time tomorrow, Jenkins."

As always he had the final word.

Dundee   April 1899

THE OLD MAN AND THE C

Roddie McKenzie

Jamie MaCallum looked across the noon twilight of the
spinning flat through the slanting sunbeams made visible by
the stoor of jute dust that hung in the air; it made his clothes
stink and scratched the back of his throat. Near the end of
the hall he identified his fifteen year-old pal, Paddy McAnn.
Jamie sighed and returned to collecting the jute yarn coiling
like demented tentacles around the twirling bobbins. He
removed a full rack of bobbins, reached to the box at his
feet and inserted an empty one. Another ten minutes before
the lunch time bummer would shriek and they would be on
their way.

Within a few seconds of the bummer's howl, the framer
machinery clattered rheumatically to a halt - a moment's
silence and the women and girls` chatter echoed in the stillness
of the mill, spiralling up to the cast iron hammer beams.

Jamie followed a few steps behind Paddy into the
warehouse; Paddy was already pulling aside a dank bale of
jute to retrieve two canvas kitbags.

"Ye huv the food and drink eh telt ye tae get? Enough
for three days o` hiding oot?" Jamie whispered. Paddy
nodded. Passing the window on the way to the cast iron

staircase at the end of the floor, they paused and gazed down from the heights the Dens Mill stood on.

Above the warehouses around Victoria Dock they could see the masts of the clippers, their sails furled against the scaffolding of the upper spars. Jamie nudged Paddy and they began to descend the stairs hoping that the dull clunk of their footfalls would not attract the attention of the overseer, or of the warehousemen. Slipping out of the loading bay past the big Clydesdales nodding in the shafts of the carts, they were quickly out of the gate and down the brae. Free.

They felt the warm glow of the April sunshine on their backs as they turned onto the cobbles of Dock Street. Seagulls swooped and squawked like grating metal overhead. They could see a line of barques and clippers tied up along the quayside. As they passed the great barn of the Dundee East railway station, with its semicircular roof and attendant square sentinel entrance columns, a shrill whistle behind them caused them to glance over their shoulders and step aside rapidly as a shunting pug puffed laboriously up behind them; it was a short train of four wagons and it passed quickly on its way to the Western harbours, leaving two straight parallel trails of sparkling steel.

"We hae tae find where the *Polar Star* is berthed," Jamie said, glancing around the quayside. Paddy`s lack of response caused him to turn and catch his friend`s reluctant eye.

"Ye`re no haein second thoughts again Paddy? Eh thoat we hud been through a this afore. Dae ye no want tae mak yer fortune? We'll mak mair on a single voyage than five years in thon mill- *and* some adventures. Or wid ye rather end up as a kettle biler, makin yer Ma`s denner fur the rest of yer life when they pit ye oot the door o the mill?"

"Eh *dae* want tae get oan the boat, but eh hae aa ma family here, ye…" Paddy stopped short of alluding to Jamie`s orphant status.

"We'll only be awa seven months. Onywey, wiz it no just yesterday ye were moanin aboot how ye were seek o her bossing ye aboot?"

"Aye…but ye are sixteen."

"Aye but nuttin. Dinnae be a fairdeegowk! We wid probably get the boot frae Baxter`s onywey when they find we left the Mill withoot permission. So nae mair haverin. Let`s find that boat an get oorsels stowed awa."

Jamie strode forward to the dock entrance, head up, squinting in the sunlight, kitbag of worldly belongings bumping against his back. Paddy slunk along a few steps behind, eyes to the ground for reasons other than shielding them from the golden dazzle in the cloudless cerulean sky.

After a fruitless hour searching the Victoria and Camperdown docks and creeping around to avoid the carters from the mill, who were loading bales from the dockside sheds, they were no closer to finding the *Polar Star*. Despondent, back on Dock Street, the westerly breeze brought a faint ammonia whiff of fish from the Green Market, as Jamie had an idea.

"We need tae ask a seafarin man. They wid ken where the

Polar Star would be. That`s it! The Seaman`s Hame - jist alang the street." He indicated the angular building, topped by a rounded cupola. "They're bound tae ken!"

With Paddy in pursuit, Jamie half-ran across the cobbles slowing as he came up to the door of the coal-smoke-blackened sandstone building. A man in his fifties sat in a battered chair by the doorway, puffing contentedly on his clay pipe. He observed Jamie through an aromatic fog. Jamie took in his faded waist coat, battered mariner`s hat and shirt sleeves rolled up to reveal faded blue tattoos on his muscular arms.

"Aye, ye`re in a fair stramash, young maister. Wid ye be looking for somebody?"

"Aye!" Jamie replied. "We were looking fur a sailor mannie, someone wha would ken whaur the *Polar Star* wid be found."

"Yer faither`s oan the whalers then?"

"Nut," Paddy interjected, "we're going to sea oorsels."

The man blew out a long stream of blue smoke and gestured to them with the stem of his pipe.

"Ah-ha, so ye will be mariners then?"

"Nut, we`re mill.. OW!"

Jamie elbowed Paddy in the ribs, turned towards him and glared.

"We would be much obliged if you tell us where tae find the *Polar Star*, Sir."

The man laughed and tapped out his pipe against the leg of the chair.

"Och yer keen tae be aff tae sea richt enough; eh ken ye whaling men are affy impatient, but if ye will stand an auld fellow seaman a drink eh`ll tell ye whit dock yer ship lies in."

"Aye, we wid be happy tae dae that, Sir."

"Ma pals call me Toshie. Ye`ll hae a drouth on yersells if ye've been dashing aboot the docks on such a braa day. C`moan, 'Nancy`s' is jist twa doors up."

He rose unsteadily and walked awkwardly up the street with Jamie and Paddy following. Ahead to their left, the great Gothic arch obscured the sailing boats moored in the Earl Grey Dock and the western sky was pierced by the spectacular baronial spike of the West Railway Station building.

They reached a sun-bleached wooden door in the cliff of a nearby tenement. Toshie pulled it open and they were inside a dank room smelling of stale beer and piss. Inside a dozen gaunt faces turned, eyes blinking in the sudden shock of sunlight. They gazed for a moment, nodded briefly and returned to their murmured conversations. The barman, a rotund bear of a man, turned and welcomed the newcomers.

"Hello Toshie, nice tae see ye. How`s yer leg for woodworm the day? Hae ye siller, man?"

"Och ye ken me fine, Angus. I`m aye guid fur a wee refreshment, but these fine sea-gangin men are standing me a wee drink."

"Aye...Aye, eh see. Whit will ye gentlemen be having then?"

"Weel then, maybe eh`ll have a wee hauf and a half pint."

"And fur the ither gentlemen?"

Paddy looked askance while Jamie seized the moment.

"Twa pints o yer best barman please," (having heard this said in his begging days in the taverns of Lochee).

Angus seemed to take an eternity before finally clasping a meaty hand onto the beer pump. Jamie was struck by the smell of stale tobacco but was entranced by the way the big man was able to fill the pint glasses, one–handed, while discussing the shipping and reaming out his gaping hawse-pipes of nostrils with a finger of his free hand, absent-mindedly flicking his findings onto the sawdust covered floor.

"Tak a seat, gentlemen." Angus indicated the tired rattan bar stools.

As the drinks were banged clumsily onto the greasy, stained pinewood bar, slopping their murky foaming contents over the lip of the glasses, Paddy had a revelation.

"Toshie? Toshie McIntosh? *Ye* are Toshie McIntosh - the man that survived three weeks in an open boat when ye were lost at sea. Eh`m richt am a no? Ma Da telt me about you - he read it in T*he Advertiser.* Ye had tae eat yer hat and the jack aff the main sprit tae keep alive till thon Danish fishermen rescued ye."

Toshie sighed and sank uneasily onto a bar stool. When they were all seated, he went on. "Aye lad, yer richt. That`s me, poor auld Toshie - lost baith legs tae the Arctic cauld. Eh could tell ye a tale aboot the frozen seas richt enough."

Jamie interjected petulantly, "Ye were gonnae tell us where tae find the *Polar Star.*"

"Aa in guid time laddie, but mebbe eh kin tell ye a wee

bit aboot ma whaling then ye kin tell me aboot yours." Jamie gulped and fidgeted on his stool.

Toshie continued. "Aye it wis the Spring bank holiday of May 1884. Och, did we no have a braa send off - aw the lads were there doon oan the Earl Grey dock waving; wimmen and lassies tossing oranges and red herrins, for luck, tae their men leaning oan the taffrail as the *Chieftain* got under way. At that time eh hid been eighteen year in the whaling - sterted as a laddie at fourteen - and by that time I wiz a linesman. We were hoping fur a guid season`s hunting, as '83 hadna been much o`a year, but the price o` baleen had jumped again and we were all in guid cheer- some mair than ithers. Maist o` the lads were fu - ye`ll ken whit eh mean?" He nudged Jamie and laughed. Then his brow furrowed and he sighed heavily.

"But little did we ken that we wid lose fower ships - aye - the *Star, Resolute, Triune and Jan Mayen* - aye, and some o` my mates from the *Chieftain* - afore the season wiz through." He downed his whisky in one.

"We made the Arctic Ocean without ony mishaps and then on March 26th, we were east of Greenland and Captain Gellatly - being a new commander and keen as a knife - wiz in the craw's nest. Suddenly we heard him bellowin, "A fall! A fall! ...thirty degrees off the port bow."

"Weel - ye`ll ken yersel - we were racing ontae the deck, pulling on whatever clothing we had handy and scrambling intae the whale boats. Lads were barely aboard but they were lowering the boats doon as the ship gave way. Gellatly nearly fell aa the wey doon the mast and got intae his boat and we were awa pullin like maniacs, for tae port we could see twa spouts like fountains rising oot o the troughs of the waves. Efter a chase of aboot twenty minutes, Gellatly`s harpooner let aff the gun and speared the hindermaist whale, a bottlenose he wiz." He paused for another pull of his half empty beer.

"He didnae run fur lang before Gellatly`s boat was alangside as he tired and they pit the lances intae him and he wiz done. They secured him and rowed back tae the *Chieftain* and made the whale fast tae the starboard. Meanwhile we pulled hard for hours efter the ither one trying tae keep aff his eye, so he widna tak fright. Eventually after anither half day, Taylor in oor boat harpooned him and the chase wiz really on. Meanwhile Gellatly had picked up some provisions and his boat cam back tae assist us - the fast boat. By the time he got there the whale was deid. Man ! We were tired frae the rowin and the cauld, but jubilant, ken... and that`s when it went wrang."

Toshie fell silent and inched his sud-stained empty glass to the bar. Paddy looked at Jamie and Jamie put his hand into his pocket. Suitably refreshed, Toshie continued. "It wiz like a heavy curtain had been let doon frae the skies - ye couldna see beyond the ither boats and of the *Chieftain*? Nothing!

"Twa boats stayed wi the whale and the ithers looked fur the *Chieftain* but couldna find her. The fourth boat capsized and a lad wiz drooned. Efter righting the boat, eh was transferred to her. That wiz when ma luck failed me, for when the boats separated on the 30th, Gellatly and Taylor made Iceland after fifty hours and the third boat wiz picked up by a Danish vessel. But oor boat…weel. We were pulling fur Iceland too, but efter three days without food or drink Wully McGregor began tae drink seawater. Bad idea that wiz, as ye`ll ken yersells. Then Wully threw the compass overboard and Iceland became problematical. The next day Wully bit Alex  the harpooner oan the leg, yellin` aboot roast beef, before he drapped doon stone deid." Paddy stared in horror and Jamie twisted on his stool.

"The cauld, the thirst and the hunger took its toll and within twa days, Jamie Cairns and Wully Christie deid on us and me and Alex , exhausted as we were, pit them ower the side. Ma legs were swollen tae twice their size wi the frostbite and Alex wiz exhausted. We drifted - eh dinnae ken fur how lang - and when eh woke up, poor Alex wiz deid. Man! Eh felt the loneliest man in the world and eh wished fur death masel."

"But ye won through - ye survived." Jamie was on the edge of his stool. He noticed Toshie`s glass sparkled once more, while Toshie seemed to be scratching his moustache absent mindedly.

"Aye, eh won through, but at a price. It wiz anither twa weeks afore the Danes picked me up and they had tae amputate ma legs. Er, lads, eh appear tae be financially embarrassed. It seems eh left ma pooch in ma ither troosers. Eh`ll gang tae the hoose and then we kin finish meh tale."

Jamie was anxious to get out to find their boat. He signalled to Angus, who dutifully re-filled Toshie`s glasses. The boys had barely touched theirs.

"Fur days we drifted. Eh couldnae bear tae put Alex ower the side - so lonesome eh wiz and so hungry.. so hungry…"

"Eh, but ye ate yer hat and the jack aff the bowsprit - tae survive. Ma Da telt me."

"Mebbe aye, mebbe no… but there's no a lot o feeding in a hat. Besides eh needed it tae keep frae losing ma lugs tae the cauld, an there was anither source o victuals. Eh realised efter a hungry week…."

Jamie's eyes bulged, his tongue was sticking to his palate and he could only stutter a short message.

"Ye couldnae…he wiz yer shipmate. It…it wisnae Christian…ye didnae. YE DIDNAE!"

Toshie spoke softly and motioned to Jamie to sit down.

"Whit wiz eh tae dae laddie? Ma strength wiz gone, eh couldnae pit him ower the side. Besides, Alex wiz a man that traded in deid bodies - o whales mark ye - he would huv understood though. A body`s nae use tae ye when ye`re deid…. Och, but being whaling lads ye`ll ken sometimes ye huv tae dae what`s necessary in a tight spot. It's no uncommon in the whaling trade. Onywey, enough of ma havers… Ye`ll find the *Polar Star* in Earl Grey Dock, second dock after the Arch. Noo, huv ye time tae tell me ane o yer whaling tales afore ye mak for yer ship?" But the white-faced boys were already in hushed conference and seemingly, in agreement.

"Nut, sorry Mr Toshie, sir. We hae some pressing business."

"Ach too bad, eh'll mebbe hear yer tales when ye get back. Angus here wiz just telling me Stephen's wiz looking fur apprentices- eh wundered whether ony o yer shore-bound pals might be interested in that? Guid money eh hear- and a trade fur life."

Paddy was drifting to the door. Jamie slung his bag to his shoulder.

"Stephen's shipyaird alang the shore, ye say? Lads o oor age? I can pass it on.... and thanks, sir." And the lads bundled themselves out the door.

As they hurried up Dock Street, Jamie was insistent. "Eh dinna believe him - he's makin' it up. Nut - he's MAKIN' IT UP, Paddy!"

Paddy stopped.

"Jamie... meh bag...eh've left meh bag.... Jamie, eh dinnae hae meh bag."

"Weel, ye had better gang back and get it." He shook his stunned pal. "Paddy! Paddy!"

Paddy stared, jaw slack, silent, then, mouth oscillating like a goldfish's, he turned and ran back down to the pub door. He furtively slipped inside and found his bag at the brass foot rail.

Toshie and Angus were convulsed with laughter. They hadn't noticed him scooping up his kitbag. Angus's blubbery frame shook.

"Och, Toshie, yer a richt twister...the way ye played those laddies...eh hud tae bite ma hand at times."

"Weel an auld legless sailor has tae be clever tae stay

legless - if ye ken ma meaning. Besides the whales are gone, the trade is finished. There's been enough young stowaways in an icy grave."

"An that bit aboot eating poor Alex…"

Toshie's eyes narrowed, as cold and hard as harpoon tips.

"Eh, Angus, but jist mebbe if eh had a man o yer generous constitution in the boat wi me, eh could have made Iceland wi ma legs intact."

Paddy backed silently to the door, but there was a loud crack as he stood on a discarded T-bone. Toshie and Angus swivelled their heads in unison. Transfixed in their searchlight gaze, Paddy fled out the door before another word could be said.

TWO FOR THE PRICE OF ONE

Faye Stevenson

It happened that I had been passing through the office when the call was received. Such excitement. Margaret Mather, one of our volunteers, had been asked to take part in a local radio programme: 'Ordinary People, Extraordinary Lives', they called it. It was to take place here, at Grey Lodge. I had to seize the moment. Surely there could be no-one more extraordinary than Miss Walker? I was determined that her story should be told.

A gale was blowing up the Hilltown as I emerged from the front door of Walker House. I hoisted, ever so slightly, my long black skirt and petticoats. I was in a hurry, you see. The important visitor was due at Grey Lodge and I was most anxious to be there. I stopped suddenly as a pair of dusty, old boots soared past my eyes and walloped the ground beside me.

"Joseph! What are you doing?" I asked

The owner, still wearing the boots, picked himself up and grinned.

"Sorry, Ethel. Didna see ye. I wis swinging."

"*There is no swing!*" I remonstrated. "*And it's Miss Henderson to you, Master Thomson.*"

It was not the first time that I had had to chastise Joseph for his familiarity.

"*Where are you going? Not to Grey Lodge I trust?*"

"*Aye.*"

"*Run off and play. You will only be a hindrance to me.*"

"*Nut! I wis here lang afore you,*" Joseph spat his reply.

I composed myself. He was a young boy after all. "*You may have been here, in spirit, before me, but I lived in the big house. I belong here. You, on the other hand, strayed in. And stayed.*"

"*Och, drap deid, Ethel!*"

"*In case you haven't noticed Master Thomson, we are dead!*"

Joseph wailed, as he always did, when reminded of this obvious fact.

"*Ye dinna like me, Miss Henderson, dae ye?*" he sobbed, wiping his nose on his sleeve in one long motion from the elbow to the cuff.

"*Nonsense, Joseph. You may not have been the most agreeable companion at times but I have been most appreciative of your presence nonetheless.*"

"*Is that nut ye dinna or aye ye dae?*"

As always when dealing with Joseph, I found myself relenting. "*You may stay for a while. Speak only when you are spoken to and don't interrupt me when I am talking. Agreed?*"

Joseph nodded. The sky above me began to rumble; small, busy rain clouds were amalgamating. The tall, grey 'Multis' leaned over like giant tombstones, as if to eavesdrop on our conversation. I quickened my pace.

"It is imperative, Joseph, that you allow me to concentrate, if I am to have any influence over the proceedings."

"I dinna ken how, Miss Henderson. They canna hear or see us."

He was correct of course. I had no plan - other than trying to make my presence felt. I did, however, have every confidence in Margaret. She probably knew more about Grey Lodge than anyone else (alive that is).

We slipped quietly into Grey Lodge's Green Room. We were late. Margaret was there already; calm and assured. A few seats from her sat a young woman whom I assumed to be the presenter. She scanned through some documents on her knee, pausing every few seconds to scribble some notes in the margins. I stopped before them and smiled. Joseph stood to attention by my side. It required two coughs to remind him to doff his cap. In turn I straightened my grey cape. My Mother used to say it was too big for my small frame and appeared to weigh me down but it had been gifted to me by Miss Walker before she died. I wore it on the day of her funeral, Thursday 3rd July 1913, when at the gates of Balgay Cemetery I bade her farewell.

I pressed my fingers to my temples and felt for any loose strands that might have fallen from beneath my hat. As for Joseph, I tried not to be so disapproving but from his moth eaten cap down to the shabby leathers on his size eight feet, my gaze lingered longer than was necessary. He rubbed his boots alternately on the back of his socks.

"Sorry to have kept you waiting," the woman said. She

stretched over and shook Margaret's hand warmly. "Stella Haldane. Caledonia F.M."

At least I hadn't missed anything of importance although Stella's next remark caught me unawares. She suggested that the interview might be conducted at the Queen's Hotel in the Nethergate. I had not anticipated such an option.

"This rather reminds me of a doctor's waiting room. My team won't be here until this afternoon. That gives us plenty of time to plan what we can leave in or take out. It would be more comfortable and I could buy you lunch on my expenses. What d' you think?"

If they moved to another venue I would have no control. I must confess I panicked. I stood up abruptly. Joseph took this as an indication to panic also. He leapt on to the coffee table in the centre of the room and swivelled around as if he had just been caught plundering apples and was seeking an escape route. From there he sprang on to a chair next to Stella. But as he landed, he disturbed some of her papers. As the top sheet fluttered to the ground, Joseph raced along the seats to the window where he turned and shouted, *"Have they seen us?"*

I knew then that he had no concept of what had caused my anxiety. Inadvertently his actions had caused Stella to reconsider. Apparently, when Joseph turned to face me, he had snagged the drapes. Stella had assumed the strong wind had blown the curtain causing her notes to slip. When she rose to look out the window, the weather outside had worsened.

"Let's take a rain check," she joked. "We'll get soaked if

we go out in that."

Joseph was as confused as I. Never before had either of us been able to make an object move. Or perhaps we had and had not been aware of it.

Stella's finger zigzagged over Margaret's questionnaire. I knew they shouldn't have, but her red nails intrigued me. Often, I felt as if my old world had lacked colour.

Stella spoke up. "Before we begin, can I confirm some details? Margaret Mather. Born 18th January 1937 making you....."

Seventy!" cheered Joseph. *"I've aye been guid at countin."*

Margaret hooted when Stella said that she thought she looked much younger. To me, with her shoulder length hair and pencil-lined lashes, Margaret had remained unchanged for decades. She also worried that her life had not been remarkable enough to warrant the interest shown by Caledonia. Stella convinced her otherwise.

"It started here," said Margaret lifting her hands and face towards the ceiling; her eyes smiled appreciatively. "A shy fifteen year old. Grey Lodge gave me the impetus and opportunity. What can I say? I love it as much now as I did then."

Stella admitted she'd never heard of Grey Lodge until Margaret's file had landed on her desk. That was what I had hoped for. Miss Walker's story would be heard at last.

Margaret continued, "It's a community education centre for young and old. This used to be St Margaret's Hostel. It's changed such a lot since I first came. Not just the building but the folk too. It was strict. Not like now. You couldn't wander around as you pleased. You wouldn't dare. The warden lived upstairs. Blanche…Blanche Whitton. I came along when my mother moved from the Overgate to the Wellgate. It was the youth club that attracted me, especially the themed party nights." Margaret laughed. "I went as an Oxo girl once."

I willed Margaret to talk of Miss Walker, of those exhilarating times: the changes, the reforms. Professor Ewing. Professor D'Arcy Thompson. They were middle class philanthropists and Miss Walker was at the forefront, never afraid to speak her mind, wouldn't accept no for an answer. And I was there too, taking notes, typing letters to the elite of Dundee. I would accompany Miss Walker to the restaurants in the Hilltown and at Maxwelltown and then onto the Social Union meetings. Patrick Geddes, my benefactor, and the other Professors would be there, discussing how they would raise the money to keep the two new restaurants going and what could be done to persuade the jute owners to give new mothers more time off work.

"Joseph! I need your help."

A photograph of Miss Walker with some of the professors hung on the wall near the door. If it moved, then perhaps they would discuss it. Joseph jumped up and tried to thump the frame with the palm of his hand. Nothing happened. I urged him to keep on trying; to find the same emotions he had felt earlier. Nothing. My own attempts were fruitless.

"Did your interest in music and drama begin here?"

Stella asked.

"Undoubtedly," Margaret replied. "We had a thriving group - and great fun too."

I leaned towards Joseph and whispered, *"The D.S.U initiated this, providing recreational activities for the poor, educating the person as a whole. I was most surprised to find that the shop boys and girls who attended our Dramatic Society had feelings and aspirations similar to my own. Many saw the working class as a race apart believing that the demon drink was the root of their poverty."*

"Ma faither liked a guid drink an ma granpa an aa," Joseph confessed.

"But it wasn't their fault, Joseph. Miss Walker said it was not intemperance or thriftlessness that caused such wretched misery but the lack of nutritious food and unsanitary living conditions." I patted his hand gently.

"Ma gran said that if you threw ma granpa on a bonfire he'd licht up the hale o Dundee... fir a week or mair!"

Margaret told Stella of her involvement with the Dundee Junior Showtime insisting that interest was as strong today as it was in 1970 when she established the group. They had performed at The Little Theatre in Victoria Road, the Caird Hall and they had even sung for the Queen. Margaret wrote all her own material. One of her heritage plays, 'Stoor in their Hair', had been staged at the Edinburgh Festival.

Stella thumbed through the pages. "It says here you were brought up in an orphanage?"

The youngest of fifteen, Margaret had been put up for adoption. She had spent most of her formative years alone, in residential homes; firstly in Duncarse on Blackness Road then latterly at Armistead Home in Broughty Ferry.

"I was illegitimate, you see."

As if she had sensed the gasps from Joseph and me, Margaret swiped the air above her with a nonchalant flick.

"I can say it now. It bothered me once, not now. It was a stigma all those years ago."

Stella agreed that times had indeed changed. She herself was chief bridesmaid at her parents' wedding. We listened intently as Margaret recounted her childhood experiences.

"We always walked in pairs, two by two. The corridors were long and narrow. I was a timid bairn, always afraid. Nobody took the time to explain. We ate off a laundry basket; it was our table. We were in the basement, I think. It was during the war. Our beds were old mattresses on the floor and there was only one cot. Each night we moved up a mattress until it was your turn for the cot."

"Did you have any visitors?" Stella asked tentatively.

"Never. At visiting time, I had to sit beneath a large rocking horse. I can only remember their feet - the visitors. At the end, everyone had to line up. One of the nurses would wait with a trolley. If you received anything you had to put it on the trolley for sharing. I longed to have something to put on it, but never did."

"Did you ever go out?"

"Oh yes. Several times. For check ups at the Children's Shelter in Dudhope Street. Mr Fisher was the Children's Officer. You stood on a table, stripped to your pants. It was like a conveyor belt. No explanations. People taking notes, looking for signs of abuse. Rat bites. Bruises." Margaret let out a long sigh.

"Imagine yer Ma no wantin ye," groaned Joseph

I thought about telling Joseph of my own mother's dilemma but I knew he would not have understood. After father died, Professor Geddes persuaded Miss Walker to take me on as one of her assistants. Mother was struggling to support my brothers through university. Miss Walker would have preferred an older girl, I know, but I'm sure I fulfilled my obligations. I remained at Walker House for ten years until I succumbed to smallpox at the age of twenty-five.

I, too, abandoned a child once, in a tenement slum. Miss Walker had entrusted me with the book keeping at the Maxwelltown restaurant. I had to record meticulously the visit of every mother and child who came for support. These nursing mothers were provided with a hot, nutritious meal on the condition that they would have their babies weighed and they would not return to work. It was 2d for mothers who could afford to pay; for others, it was free. On one occasion, at Mary Walker's insistence, I had to find one of the women, Agnes Glen, who had failed to return. I had visited homes before to collect rent on behalf of the Social Union - but only in the Hilltown area. The Westport was unfamiliar to me.

It was late afternoon. The close was dark and quiet. I edged my way up the steps to the first landing. I heard a child cry. Not a loud wail but a fatigued whimper. The door was open a smidgen. I called out for Agnes but there was no reply. I pushed the door further. It was so sudden - the stench. Excrement, dampness, sea, sick, smoke, ale. The odours constricted my breathing. I had to swallow my bile. A fish crate on the floor contained the infant. As I cradled her in my arms, a large shadow on the box bed belched.

A gruff voice called out, "Aggie? Yer early. Get in an I'll warm ye up."

I left the child and flew.

Stella was asking about Margaret's mother now.

"She came for me, eventually," Margaret confirmed. "I didn't know what a mother was, how could I? This woman took me on a bus; the first time on a bus for me. We went to a house in Tay Street Lane." Margaret shuddered. "Rats ran over my face as I slept."

"Was it like that for you, Joseph?" I asked.

"Wis it hell. I lived at the posh end: Swanky Land, No 33. A lot posher than ma Gran's hoose at Gaity. We had runnin water an a washie hoose ootside. Ma Gran came tae dae her washin an aa. The rent wis 5/9d a week." He waited for my reaction. *"I telt ye it wis posh!"*

I sensed the interview was winding down when Margaret began questioning Stella about her career as a journalist. They chatted about their first jobs. Margaret had earned thirty-two shillings per week working in a shoe shop. There had been no mention of Miss Walker at all.

"Had you...survived, Joseph, what occupation do you think you would have undertaken?" I tried to sound interested.

"Onythin tae dae wi horses s'pose. I wis aye up the farmyard at Peter's Pend. The coos wid get drunk on the 'draught' the lorries brocht in fae Ballingall's Brewery. It wis funny. I wanted tae be a fireman like ma Uncle Boab. They hyded at the corner o Ward Street in the firemen's hoosies. Sometimes he let me feed the horses. That's how I ended up here. I wis doon at Bell Street Station when word came in there wis a fire at David Walker's bakery, up near ma bit. I wis that busy runnin back tae Bonnethill, I didna notice the horses ahint me. Next I kent, I wis in the big gairden at Grey Lodge. That's why I started comin, tae get a shot o' yon big swing. I mind o you, Ethel. Ye were affy bonnie 'pared wi the rest o the auld, fat wimmin.'

I put a motherly arm around him and we sat in companionable silence. A genial pensioner popped his head around the door. It was John Lynch.

"Kettle's on if ye fancy a wee cuppa," he hollered.

Margaret suggested that Johnny might be a suitable guest for another time. He'd been a professional boxer with several prestigious titles to his name. As John closed the door, the most unexpected thing happened. Miss Walker's picture fell to the floor. Stella picked it up and asked who they were.

"That's Mary Lily Walker with the founders of the D.SU," said Margaret. "I suppose you could say she was Dundee's first Social Worker. A voice for the poor. That's why she set up Grey Lodge." Then she pointed out Miss Walker's house from our window; the sun shone on the solid stone building.

"What's the D.S.U?" Stella asked.

"The Dundee Social Union," Margaret began, "was founded in 1888…"

"To promote the well being of the inhabitants of Dundee," I chorused, *"not limited by class, religion or condition."*

Joseph clapped and whistled approvingly.

"Good afternoon. This is Stella Haldane with the second programme in our series, 'Ordinary People, Extaordinary lives'. I'm broadcasting from Scotland's first Social Settlement, Grey Lodge, at the heart of the Hilltown in Dundee. Today, I have two remarkable stories to tell…"

'Whaur ye goin, Ethel? It's nae feenished.'

"It is for us," I laughed. *"Come, Joseph! Let's go to the garden. You can teach me how to swing."*

MALLET

John Mooney

We were at the fifth hole, the ain wi the coo's hent leg goin to the richt, and oor porter, that's what we call them, stood astride the ball wi Cleek in his hand, looking doon the lang green-ribboned fairway tae the white flag. Now Cleek was a braw player. Some fowk, especially the young ins, might say he was a braw club but whit did they ken? In this situation, however, I could see he was the wrang player tae use.

You see Bulger had driven us aff the tee a guid 220 yards and that left another 160 to reach the green. Now the porter had chosen Cleek, which wasn't a bad choice normally, but he hadnae noticed that the wind had come roon ahent us so if Cleek hit the ball as we knew he could he would be at least ten to twenty yards too lang, way past the flag. Course you canna blame the porters for that. They're no meant to think. So we had to sort this oot.

"Richt gaither roond," I said tae the other players in the bag, "we have to make him play Jigger."

Jigger, ye see, is a player wi a steeper angle tae his face and would normally be expected to carry 130 maybe 140 yards an straight, but wi this wind blawin doon the fairway Jigger could mak it to the green nae bother. Now this disnae

141

ay work but it wis oor job, oor responsibility if ye like, tae try an mak it happen for oor porter, an it's been like that fir mair than fower hunder years.

So we gets intae the huddle, then we starts "Jigger,Jigger,Jigger, Jigggggger ..."

I canna tell you why this works. All I can say is that it's been done like this since Queen Mary's time. That's the ain that came ower frae France.

Suddenly, the porter walks ower tae the bag, puts Cleek in an taks oot...Jigger! He swings Jigger in the air, doon tae the ba then smack, the ba's high in the air fleeing doon the fairway, across the burn, past the bunkers, then drops, spinning backwards, to land ahent the flag aboot five yards past. Then it starts tae run backwards towards the flag an stops jaist twa fut short. Now that brocht a smile tae the porter's face. Shots like that mak my job very easy. Ye see I'm a putter, a putter wi a head the shape o a mallet. That's why I'm called Mallet.

When we got back to the big hoose oor porter, wi his hairy troosers tucked into his checked stockings and his creaky brogues on his feet, went through his usual rigmarole. The bag was carefully placed in the corner o' the hall under the stag's heid and facing the auld grandmother clock. Hairy troosers opened the frosted glass door and walked doon the lang corridor wi his echoing clumpy steps in time wi the clock. Tick-tock, tick-tock, clump-clump, clump-clump a' the way doon tae the scullery to get a cloth to wash doon oor faces. Then tick-tock, clump-clump a' the way back.

One by one we were taken oot the bag, washed doon wi the cloth and laid oot on the cauld black and white tiles like soldiers lying to attention. Then, as he aye does, he picks us up one at a time, gives us a guid looking over and we're a' put back in the bag again.

This is whit I think is the best part of the day, when we're no playing that is. The hoose goes quiet, then just afore the sun goes doon it keeks through the glass diamonds at the tap o the door and ye kin see the dust rising blue an dusky pink, then the moon does the same job and it gets even bluer and quieter.

That particular night Hairy Troosers brought a parcel in an laid it alangside us. It wis lang an thin, wrapped in broon paper opened at the tap whaur the string had come loose. I had expected this for a while noo. The fact is we had a bit o a tragedy no lang ago. One o oor players, Bulldog he was called, well he wis…taken back. Tae let ye understand, that's the worst thing that can happen tae a player. Ye see he started to blame the porter for some shots that went aglee. Well once ye start that it's a clear sign he just wasna goin tae mak it. It's no everybody that has it in them tae dae the job. He was taken awa an…well he was never heard o again.

"Hello, is Mr Mallet there?" The question came frae the opening at the tap o the parcel.

"Aye," I said, "I'm Mallet. Have you come frae Mr Gourlay?"

"Yes," the parcel said, "from Mr Gourlay of Carnoustie, Clubmaker of distinction, Clubmaker extraordinary,

Clubmaker supreme…"

"Extraordinary he is," I interrupted, "and what do ye ken about us here in Barry?"

"Only that you are the most experienced and best putter in the whole of Scotland and Angus and the world, sir, and the one that will help me win The Championship," came the reply.

"Well we dinna speak about The Championship here, laddie. We're here to help porters enjoy the gemme o' golf, no to win championships…necessarily." The last word was said almost inaudibly. "And anyway it's sets of players and teamwork that win championships, no individuals." I couldn't help adding, "Especially a brassie."

"A brassie?" questioned the parcel.

"Aye, why did you think the man put a brass plate on yer heid?"

Well, it looked like I was richt enough. The porter had gone to see Mr Gourlay and got a replacement for Bulldog, a brassie.

"Right then, Brassie, you had better meet the rest of the gang. There's Jigger here, he gets us from the fairway on to the green aright. Just shak yer heid Jigger. Then there's Bulger, he gets us started aff the tee. And we've got Cleek, Mashie and Spoon, they're the lads to get us oot o' any trouble in between. And then of course there's oor specialists. That's One Eyed Jock, him wi the hole in his heid, he gets us oot o water. Ye see the water runs oot through his heid and the rest o him hits the ball. And there's oor niblick Flower Face, she's bonnier than the rest and spends most of her time in the sand. An wait till the sun's up before ye ask why she's caud Flower Face."

I could see the puzzled look on his face when he started to speak. "So where do you think I fit...?"

"Good night Brassie," I said maybe a wee bit abruptly, but if he was one o us now, he had to learn right away who was the gaffer. We would see in the morn if he was any guid. Aye, we had work to do.

Next morning, astride the porter's back, we followed the Barry Burn as it murmured doon tae the links, a mild, harmless wee burn that would soon turn wicked and spiteful as it snaked through the gowf course on its way tae the sea.

We were hanging aboot at the starter's box waiting oor turn when the porter walks over wi Brassie still in his wrapping. He taks the paper aff and that's when we realised what Brassie was. We all sucked in an held oor breath. It was Flower Face that recovered first.

"Oh my goodness!" she whispered. "Look...look...it's ...he's no...he's no hickory!"

The rest o the lads, aye myself included, could only stand and stare. Not only was he no hickory but he was shining like a mirror. He was dazzling. And he looked like he was enjoying the attention. By the time we got to the fourth hole oor heids had stopped spinning roon and we were gradually quieting doon. And anyway we had Brassie's learning tae think aboot.

He was bright enough aricht and no just to look at so he

was beginning to get the idea but I saw something in his manner that troubled me. When a mistake wis pointed oot, he didna aye think he was wrang. Anyway Jigger took over the next few holes which gave me time to hae a word wi Flower Face. I could see she wasn't making her usual contribution to things and it wasn't like her. Something was bothering her. "Whit's wrang, lass?" I asked her.

She looked surprised then thoughtful then said, "Is it that obvious, Mallet?"

"Aye," I replied and waited.

"I don't know," she continued after a pause. "It's like we're moving…moving very slowly…away from something. I don't know what, and I don't know what we're moving towards, but it frightens me. It's…it's not like it used to be, Mallet." I could see her heid was starting to shake a bit so I stuck mine close in under hers.

"Look, lass, I think I ken what it is. It's change," I said. "We're all frightened of change but we canna do onything aboot it. And it's no always bad. When you came here first we had to cope wi change but we got used to it, and you. And it was a good change. Now, because o you, we're no feart o bunkers." I let that sink in a while then said, "Listen, I have some news that will cheer ye up. Now is as good a time as any to let everyone know."

I could see we had just finished the ninth hole so it was the time the porters went aff to the tea hut. I liked this part because it meant we could get aa the news frae the other players whilst we waited. We had been set doon on the ground, leaning against the hut so before anyone else arrived I called for a huddle.

"I've got a bit of news for you lot. And it's guid news. Next week," I paused to get their whole attention, "we're playing in a competition." At this announcement they started jumping up an doon an birlin their heids. "And…" I waited for their attention again, "we're playing in the Championship." At that news, the bag, wi us in it, started to rock back and forward before slowly slipping doon the side o the hut.

The day afore the Championship I had to be taken tae Mr Gourlay's workshop, roon the corner from the Links, for a wee repair. He wis a bit busy so the porter laid me doon on the bench and left. Mr Gourlay wis dealing wi a few customers so I had a guid look aboot. There wis tools hingin frae the ceilin, tools on the stoorie bench, machines an gadgets, spiders' webs, wood shavings, players' heids needing shafts and shafts needin grips and above aa the smell o leather and glue. It wis a fine chance tae catch up wi any news cos Mr Gourlay aye had a bit o a crack wi the customers.

I listened fascinated tae a sorts o stories aboot new players an whit could be done wi them, players that kin mak the balls go round corners, new balls wi wee holes in them, and as I listened I began to feel that winning the championship this year wasn't goin to be easy. Porters, it seemed, were beginning tae think fir themselves.

I wis pondering on this when I heard the door close. Mr

Gourlay wis standing ower me. He was neatly dressed in a shirt an tie. His short grey hair and the rimless glasses he wore perched on the end o his nose, hinted at the passing years. He wore, in contrast, a stained apron wi tools hooked intae a belt, knives keekin out o pouches an a fag was burning in his mooth. He also had the ugliest, saftest, gentlest pair o hands ye kin ever imagine.

"Weel, hallo auld freend," he said as he gently lifted me up and breathed a sigh so heavy I had the feeling I was just aboot to miss a six inch putt. "We'll no see *your* like again, noo that mallet-head putters are banned from the Championship."

The day o the Championship the whole toon joined in the parade, or so it seemed. Bunting and laddies waved from lamposts as crowds lined the streets to cheer on the Provost wi his whiskers and great chain, sodgers wi their ribbons an braw hats, coonsellers wi their importance and ahent them, the toon's barefoot ragamuffins, a' led by the kilt-swirling, drum-thumping, heids-in-the-air pipe band. Along the High Street we followed, doon Station Road and across the level crossing, on tae the Links. Crivvens, even the train tae Arbroath wi waving passengers was held up tae let us a pass.

But despite the cheers o the crowd and the rousing band, the sweetest music tae me wis the 'de ching, de ching, de ching de ching' as the players' heids knocked together as they were carried in proud procession by their porters, like archers with quivers on their backs, marching intae battle. And intae battle we went, arriving at the starter's box at the first hole.

No me, of course, though I had been put in the bag by my porter 'for auld times' sake', as he said. It was a small consolation but a bigger one to know that the others still looked to me for advice so I tried to swallow the pain for their sakes.

I called for a huddle. "Right," I began, "this isnae goin to be easy. We're goin tae be up agin some guid players but remember how guid we are. We are the best here, we kin beat anybody." Jigger, Cleek and Mashie started tae spin roon an roon. "An we're gonna play like we've never played before." One-Eyed Jock and Flower-Face joined them in a wee dance together. "We're gonna strike lang and true, we're gonna hit every flag on every green." Now Bulger, Brassie and Spoon joined in by jumping up an doon banging there heids together. "We're gonna win cos whaus like us? We're goin to win this Championship!"

We were daen a' richt until the seventeenth. Bulger got a bit ambitious an we needed One Eye tae get us oot the water, twice. Then at the last hole the burn's evil draw meant One Eye was wet again. Now when One Eye gets too much wettin, he becomes…let's say unreliable, a bit reckless even. He needs time to dry oot. So we fell behind tae tenth place but pulled back twa places efter the third roon.

So intae the last roon an we had plenty tae dae tae catch up – and yet by the time the seventeenth cam roon again, we were lying third. Bulger cleared the burn and Brassie brought us to the edge o the green wi a smasher. It wis up tae Jigger tae lay it up as near the flag as possible. But it wisna easy. He had a bunker twenty yards in front wi the flag only three foot fae the edge o the other side o bunker. He had to get the ba up an stop dead just behind the bunker wi nae room for error. Somehow he got a short backswing fae the porter and a guid follow through which clipped the ba ower the tap, doon on the green and, would ye believe it...bang against the flagpole and dropped doon intae the hole! Last hole o the Championship an we wir joint leaders. Last hole wi the burn to cross twice, an One Eye no dried oot.

The pressure was on Bulger then whoever played next. Bulger hit a beauty wi perfect position clearing the first burn hazard. But who was playing next? "We need a powerful one this time," I said as we formed the huddle. "Mashie, Mashie, Mashie!" we began. But this time, inexplicably, the centuries-auld incantation let us doon for when we got tae the ba it wis Brassie - aye Brassie! - the porter took oot the bag.

The porter let Brassie fly hitting the ba dead centre and it took aff ower the burn wi ease, safely ower an starting tae roll doon the fairway. We were a straining oor necks by this time an watched wi relief as it ran an ran an ran towards the green and straight...intae a bunker.

Weel we were still in the gemme but to force a tie wi had tae hole it frae the bunker, a bunker that ye couldna even see ower. We had one chance left an it wis up tae Flower-Face.

The porter shuffled his feet in the sand and got a guid hudd. He started intae his backswing, then stopped. Guid on ye Flower-Face, ye weren't happy wi that grip. Back it went again, then doon, doon deep, digging intae the sand an inch ahent the ba. The sand flew up in a spray an wi it a wee speck o white. The ba was wi it! It got ower the tap, came doon on the green an started tae roll towards the wee, wee hole twenty yards awa. On it went nearer, nearer, a wee swing tae the richt, then back tae the left. The twenty was now ten, then five an still it went on. Five narrowed tae three. Three became twa. It wis now inches awa. Three, twa, one it was, drappin, drappin, then…it stopped. We willed it on but it still stopped. A blade o grass was holdin it, it could still drop…but it didn't.

I prefer no tae think aboot what happened efter that. Ye try tae blank it oot. We wir feeling pretty low fir a few days, ah ken that. The sun wis shining through the diamonds intae the hall but it wisna as cheery like. The bag wis lying in its usual place, doon whaur it wis dropped but on its side, wi us lying flat. It wisna very comfy.

We must have laid like that for a week at least afore we were disturbed. We thocht we'd been forgiven but it wisnae quite that.

The bag wis picked up a richt, picked up an sat richt way up, but no by hairy troosers. No. Noo, it seemed, we'd been passed to a pair o short troosers an this time, though there wis an echoing click, it was no in time wi the clock but one beat ahead o it. Tick-tock, click-click-click, tick-tock, click-click-click, a the way tae the scullery, then tick-tock, click-click-click a the way back.

Dundee   Hogmanay, 1940
1 Year, 120 days of War
Blackout: 5.16 pm to 9.14 am

BA, BA, DA, DA!

Jane O'Neill

"Lucky First Fits! Lucky First Fits!" The man stood behind eez barrie wi eez shidders hunched an eez hands tucked up eez sleeves. Ee wiz shiverin. Ee thumped eez boots against each ither tae keep the blood movin in eez feet. "C'mon Mrs, it's Hogmanay, get yir First Fits!"

"Oh Ma, can we git lucky kippers?" Eh stood on meh tiptoes an looked ower the rows o kippers dressed in skirts made o coloured tooshie paper, their ehz like marbles, an aa starin at me!

"Ah well, Eh suppose they'll dae fir the nicht's tea," Ma said, an handed ower a tanner tae the man wha wis now blawin on eez fingers tae thaw them oot.

"Happy New Year when it comes!" ee shouted efter us

"Happy New Year tae you as well!" Ma laughed.

It's good tae see Ma laughin. Ma is happy because we dinnae hae'ah leave the twa rooms in the 'Burn efter aa an look fir a single end or a garret. Since Da left, Ma hiz been worried tae death.

Da came fae Dublin an Ma says when ee wiznae full o whisky, ee wis full o patter. Sometimes when ee came hame blind drunk, ee wid stand at the fit o the closie an mak a hell o a rackit. Ee looked richt comical wi eez hat at the back o eez heid, thumbs in eez galluses an singin at the tap o eez voice. Mrs Docherty wha lived in wir loaby wid haul up the windie an tell um tae go back tae the bog whaur ee came fae, fir it wiz in eez blood!

"Yer no in the bog noo, Thomsy Malone, so shut it. Eh've behdd in the 'Burn aa meh days," she roared, "an niver heard onythin like it."

Da wiznae scared o Mrs Docherty. Ee jist laughed. "Can you not leave a man in peace to enjoy his life. Go on and give us a tune out of your own mouth and be done with ye." Ee cerried on singin.

We've no' seen um since the summer an this wiz the cause o Ma's worry.

"Come and say cheerio to your Da, my wee treasures," ee said on the last nicht we sah him. Ee lifted me onto eez lap an kissed the back o' meh hair. "My wee pearls of beauty, me lovely children," ee said, as ee cuddled me an meh wee sisters.

Each nicht before ee went tae the barracks, Da wid kiss us but Ma wid turn awa.

"Jesus woman, are ye dead or alive?"
Ma stood wi er hands on er hips. This meant trouble.

"Thomsy Malone, the factor will be here fir the rent in the morn - just in case you forget tae come hame wi the money."

"Is it out of your mind you are, woman, to say such a 'ting. May God deny your words." Ee blessed himself twice.

"Cheerio Peggy, Cheerio Mary-Ann, Cheerio Nellie. S'long Maggie."

We ran tae the plettie tae see him go an Nellie crahled between us an stuck er hands through the railins.

"Ba Ba, Da Da!" she called, wavin both er hands.

Da didnae come back.

As the nichts passed an Da didnae come hame, Ma telt me tae look efter Mary-Ann an Nellie while she went up tae the barracks tae see if Da wiz there. When she came back she flung er headscarf an coat on the bed an sat beh the fire, runnin er hands through er hair an bitin er lip. She stared at the flames, er face glowin on the one side. When Nellie sterted tae greet she telt me tae mak er a bot'le.

"But there's no enough milk, Ma." An Nellie howled louder. Ma kept starin at the fire wi er chin in er hands. Even when the fire creaked, an the burnt coal caved in an settled, she still didnae move.

Eh gave Nellie a drap o tea in er bot'le an took er tae bed wi me an Mary-Ann. It wiz affy quiet except fir the tickin o the clock an the whistlin o the well that widnae turn aff. Then somethin queer happened. Ma sterted tae laugh. It wiz a loud cackle like a daftie, an flegged me enough tae mak me pit meh fingers in meh ears tae block oot the rackit.

It wis efter that nicht that things sterted disappearin fae the hoose. First it wiz the clock, then the wireless set, then the mantel mirror. Then ane day the men fae the brokers in the West Port came an took awa the chist o draaers fae ben the room, an the gas hoab in the kitchen. The claes were aa piled up on the bed an folded ower the bedstead. Standin wi mi ehrms folded eh gave him meh best impudent look while ee emptied the draars. The man winked at me when ee lifted the furniture an pit it on eez back.

Efter wir tea, wir neebours, Mrs Docherty an Muggie, came in an sat wi Ma an spoke aboot the predicament.

Once they were settled on the fireside chairs, eh wid git oot the bed, open the room door a wee bit and keek through the jamb an listen. If they were speakin aboot onythin interestin eh wid come through fir a drink and listen tae them gabbin. They were that busy speakin aboot the predicament they didnae notice me sittin under the table earwiggin.

"Whit a swine ee is," Mrs Docherty said aboot Da. "Imagine, up an leavin a wife an three bits o bairns withoot a hup'nae tae yer name. An ane o them no lang aff the breest! Eh tell ye, if ee sets fit in here again, eh'll mally him. Is there nae word o him yet, Maggie?"

"No, nothin. Eh went up tae the barracks every nicht fir for twa weeks, an the Sergeant says ee kens nothin. Ee shut the door in meh face."

"Aye, Thomsy Malone wiz always a bit o a fleh man, Maggie. Sittin in the pubs wi eez cronies – drinkin the whisky an stout an tellin eez fancy stories."

Muggie rocked backwards an forwards on er chair. Er

tongue flew oot an in when she got agimitated. She added, "An when ee came hame wi the whisky hunger on him, ee took the food oot the bairns' mooths."

Da never took any food oot meh mooth. Muggie wiz leein. Da brocht us a kitten fae the pet shop in the 'Burn fir us tae play wi, an it wis Ma that telt him ee wid hae'ah feed it eezsel.

"Don't be talking, woman," Da said, "sure it's only a bit of fur. Me friend Patsy in the County Mayo told me he fed his cat on nuttin atall, and it lived 'till twenty, sure it did!"

Ee went into hysterical laughin, slappin eez hand on eez knee an wipin the eh that wiz always red an wattery wi the back o eez hand.

"Weel, Maggie, dinnae say ye wurnae warned." Mrs Docherty heaved up er chist wi er big ehrms. "Nae wonder yer mither never came tae yer weddin. She wiz black affronted at er dachtir gettin merried in yon Episcopal Kirk doon Blinshall Street. Could ee no hae turned? Whit wiz the metter wi St Andra's? An him fae Dublin tae. Somethin no richt aboot that, if ye ask me."

"Thomsy said we should get married near the spot whaur we met," Ma said. "The first time eh sah him wiz in the West Port. Ee wiz singin eez hert oot tae a crood o fellas an lassies that wir goin tae the Palais fir the dancin. Ee asked me tae go wi him an eh suppose that wiz the start. That's how we got married in St Mary Magdalene's." Ma's voice sterted tae shak.

On an on they went. Yap, yap, yap, aboot Da. The next

nicht Ma had news. She wiz able tae tell Mrs Docherty an Muggie Da had pit in fir eez discharge back in April an eez papers had come through in June. Ee wiz last seen on eez own at the docks. Naebody's heard fae um since.

Eh wiz gettin cald sittin on the flare an eh wiz thinkin aboot Da. Eh sneaked back tae bed an sterted tae greet inta meh pully. Eh fell asleep thinkin aboot um singin tae Ma.

The violets were scenting the woods, Maggie,
displaying their charms to the bees.
When I first said I loved only you, Maggie,
and you said you loved only me.

The kippers were double wrapped in newspapers tae keep in the smell. Eh pit them on tap o the tatties an peas an barley an the big marra bone fir the broth. Me an Mary-Ann held the message bag between wiz an Ma cerried Nellie. It wiz Hogmanay an we were aa happy as we waaked up the Overgate tae the room an kitchen up the 'Burn.

Ma's a lot happier noo that Uncle Robert's lendin a hand. Ee's a sodger in the Black Watch. Ee signed up but ee's hame on lave fir the New Year. Uncle Robert lives up the Blackie near Mrs Lindsay wha Ma cleans fir. She's affy guid tae Ma an gied wiz a white scrubbed table fir the kitchen. Uncle Robert an eez pals brocht it tae the hoose as a favour. Ee gied Ma a new wireless an a mirror, an we've goat a gas hoab again so we dinnae hae tae cook on the fire.

Eh couldnae wait tae get hame tae help Ma wi the chores an set a new fire in time fir the bells.

Steam wiz aaplace. The pot wiz bilin on the gas an Ma gave the claes a poke every time they bubbled up in the soapy froth. The marra bone wiz cookin awa, an the kitchen smelt o meat an soap an frehd kippers. It wiz braa. Ye couldnae see in the mirror aboon the mantelpiece, or oot the windie fir the steam, an everythin wiz drippin wi watter: it wiz even runnin doon the doors. We baith had wir peenies on, an wir sleeves rolled up, while Ma lifted the steamin claes oot the pot wi the widden spane, an drapped them inta the tin basin. Eh wiz busy fillin up the black iron sink wi cald watter ready fir the rinsin. Meh hands were blue beh the time we feenished, then Ma's ehrms went roond an roond as the claes went slidin through the mangle. The claes were drehd in front o the fire on the back o the kitchen chairs.

The carrots and neeps were scraped o their dirt, chapped inta lumps then Ma slid them inta the pot with the big marra bone. Mary Ann stood on a chair at the sink an ran the watter through the peas an barley. Er frock wiz soakin doon the front an stuck tae er legs! Soon the peas an barley were in the pot an aathin goin at a rollin bile. Nellie crahled aroond the flare gettin in aabody's road an howled when the fire sterted spittin, an a spark landed on er ehrm. Ma kissed it an rubbed it wi a bit but'er, an she wiz content again.

Next we had tae iron the chair backs an doilies an press Ma's skirt an blouse. The iron wiz heatin up on the gas an eh spread the ald sheet on the white scrubbed table while Ma ripped open an ald pully case an soaked it under the runnin well. She spread it ower er green gaberdine skirt an plunged the iron ower the cloth, the steam risin an sizzlin an spittin, until the cloth wiz drehd an the skirt wiz smooth. The chores wiz aboot done. The bed in the recess wiz made, the blankets well tucked in an the pullys shoogled until they were sittin stiffly on tap o the bedspread. The flare an table wiz scrubbed clean. The sticks wiz piled up on ae side o the herth an the fender Brassoed till it wiz gleamin. The ashes wiz cleared oot the grate an the fire wiz roarin up the lum.

It had sterted rainin an Ma pinned up the blackoot curtain agin the windie an lit the gas mantle. Wir kitchen looked grand.

"C'mon an hae a wee seat you twa,' she said, an me an Mary-Ann offered tae fix er hair while she gave Nellie er bot'le. We baith sat on an ehrm o the chair an brushed an combed Ma's hair, then folded it into rolls alang the back o er neck. "Ach watch an no scart meh heid!" Ma yelled when we stuck in the hairpins tae hudd it in place! She took the sleepin Nellie through tae the bed an then rubbed wir faces wi a wet rag an goat wiz ready fir bed.

She looked in the mirror an patted baith sides o er hair. She slid red lipstick ower er lips an pit twa dots on er cheeks an rubbed it in. She smiled at ersel.

Eh lay in bed an listened tae the voice comin through the wireless.

"This is the BBC Home Service. The time is 11.30. Next, is Hame Ower Hogmanay - entertainment for everyone, followed by Big Ben at 12." I wiz determined tae bide awake an hear the bells.

At the third chime eh woke. The front door wiz bein knocked in! Mr Hitler wiz here in the 'Burn! Eh jumped up. Eh opened the door a crack an peeked through. The kitchen wiz full o khaki. Uncle Robert an eez pals filled the room each ane kissin Ma on the cheek an shakkin er hand. The scrubbed boards blackened as the watter fae their big bates spread ower the flare. The sodgers folded their toorie hats an stuffed them through the tabs on their shidders. Mrs Docherty came in wi Muggie. They pit a lump o coal in the bunker beh the sink, then settled theirsels in the fireside chairs, their hands tae the blaze. Ma ladled oot the broth inta big deep plates an set oot the chappit tatties an bits o cheese in dishes on the white scrubbed table.

The men stood aroond wi wee nip tum'lers in their hands, screwin up their faces each time they took a sip o the whisky.

"Aah!" they said in turn, an smacked their lips.

"Giez a tune on yer chanter, Robert," Mrs Docherty roared.

As Robert sterted playin, eh went back tae bed. Aabody wiz laughin an haein a guid time. Light streamed inta the bedroom an Uncle Robert wiz standin at the fit o the bed. Eh sah the red glow fae the fag in eez mooth. Eh felt the heavy weight o a great coat bein laid on the bed. It smelt o baccie an rain. He tucked the covers in richt ticht an smoothed meh hair fae meh face. Ee stood fir a minute smokin before ee went back tae the kitchen.

Eh woke when they were aa lavin. Eh tiptoed tae the door an opened it a crack again. Mrs Docherty wiz bein helped oot beh Muggie an the sodgers were bendin their heids tae get oot the door, their hats in their hands at the ready.

"Mind yer heids on the loaby gas!" Uncle Robert called, an the sodgers aa laughed.

It wiz jist Ma an Uncle Robert left in the kitchen.

"Can we open the windie a bit, Robert?"

"Better no Maggie. Ye ken it's the blackoot."

"Oh, go on Robert, open the windie jist a keek. Let the ald year oot an the New Year in."

Uncle Robert blew oot the gas mantle. Ee pit eez ehrm roond Ma's waist an she caught eez hand in hurz.

Eh closed the room door an went back tae bed.

BETWEEN THE LINES

Gaye Manwaring

As she poured the milk into her teacup, it dripped onto the letter, making the ink run in an opalescent teardrop. She blotted it with a paper napkin, angry that her carelessness had damaged something that had survived for over sixty years - three years more than herself.

The weather was nondescript with patches of desultory drizzle and glimpses of brightness. The wind was chill and she was glad to be inside the small café. The tables were covered with greasy white plastic tablecloths and adorned by small vases of yellow roses, also plastic. However the tea was good and the friendly waitress confirmed that the café had been there during the war. It seemed a lifetime ago yet that was why Ann was in Montrose with a bundle of her mother's letters to her sister.

3 February 1941

My Dear Ruth

So this is bonnie Scotland! Actually it's very beautiful when it isn't misty or raining. I love working at the Montrose Air Station. We do seem a bit remote from the war as we are involved in training rather than ops. But we still feel the effects and frustrations. I have to wear those horrid lisle stockings, as it's just too cold up here to have bare legs and draw a seam down the back with eyebrow pencil.

I really miss my Eddie, stuck on his army base in the middle of England and I can't help wondering what he's getting up to. I do hope he'll wait for me.

Your loving sister
Margaret

Now that she was actually here in Scotland, her mother's words had greater impact. Back then there must have been a constant undercurrent of fear.

12 July 1941

It would be beautiful to walk on the Montrose sands but of course the beach is off limits. Only last week a young lad was walking his dog and it ran down onto the beach and tripped a landmine. It was literally blown to bits and the poor boy found its collar thrown up onto the path with the metal studs all blackened.

There's a great little café in town where we sometimes go for a meal. But the amazing thing is that the person who oversees the kitchen there is our corporal who's in charge of the mess at the camp. Apparently he owns the place and his wife runs it during his wartime "absence". His fortuitous posting to the local aerodrome gives advantages all

round. The base gets top quality fresh food from
the local farms and the café is the only place in
town serving tinned pineapple!

Ann wondered if it could possibly be the same café. Had
any of the people walking past now known her mum during
the war? She might have sat at this very table in the 1940s
looking out at the solid red sandstone buildings. But then
the windows would have been criss-crossed with sticky
brown paper, and there would have been eight foot high
piles of sandbags at the entrance to every close.

The letters were a fascinating archive. She missed her
mum and the writings made her feel close, but some of them
raised questions. Ann wasn't sure she wanted to know the
answers.

She carefully put the letters back in her voluminous
shoulder bag, paid her bill and walked towards her car. At
the end of the wide main street there was an impressive
statue and the plaque identified the subject as Sir Robert
Peel. Her mother had talked about sitting on the plinth at
the feet of this local worthy with her friends while they ate
some chips after going to the cinema. Ann imagined the
scene – fingers burning with the heat of the chips through
the newspaper (all other paper being in short supply), noses
smarting with the tang of vinegar, and bottoms numbing on
the cold hard stone.

If she wanted to get a feel for her mother's wartime life,
she would have to go to places she knew were relevant.

Luckily the airbase where her mum had been a radio operator was now a heritage centre so she could walk round it.

At the Air Station the past crowded in. Faded photographs, eerie echoes, pieces of planes and memories of might-have-beens filled the gaps in her imagination. A scratchy Glenn Miller record put the visitors in the mood of the times. Ann subconsciously swayed her hips in time with the music. There was her mum's name (Bolton, Margaret) in the service log. She shivered. Some of the other mothers and fathers listed had not survived the war.

That gave her a twinge of guilt and she retreated to the museum's car park. Sitting in her car, looking across the airfield, she read a few more letters.

23 January 1942
One of the pilots took me up for a spin last week though it's strictly against all the rules. It was my first ever flight and it was amazing apart from the cloying smell of the high octane. The countryside looked like the farm set that Uncle Bert gave us with the lead animals and painted wooden hedges. The flight was juddery and noisy and when we stopped there was such an uncanny silence that I thought I'd gone deaf.

At least we landed safe and sound. There's a small cottage just outside the perimeter fence and its chimney stack is demolished on a regular basis. When the wind is in a certain direction the planes have to come in directly over the cottage and sometimes the pilots fly a bit too low and hit the chimney with their undercarriage. The owner has got used to it. He repairs his chimney, sends the bill to the RAF, which they pay, and waits for the next time.

Her mother had told that story to Ann and her twin, Mark, when they were children. The twins were close and agreed on many things but he was furious about her reading the letters. Mark said they were private between their mother and their aunt and reading them was as bad as grave robbing.

The next letter was written after her mother's marriage to Eddie, her father.

5 September 1942

I know Mr Churchill is right about the need for this war and I feel so patriotic when I hear him speak on the radio. But at other times I feel quite unhappy. After all we are fighting to protect our way of life, but surely this isn't what marriage is meant to be like. I hardly ever see my husband, so we can't make a home together let alone start a family. Still I'm luckier than some. One girl at the drome was devastated when her husband was badly injured abroad. He lost his right leg - and other awful injuries mean he can never become a father!

I miss my Eddie even more after our few days (and nights) together on our short honeymoon. My landlady has a ginger cat that reminds me of Eddie's red hair. Everything makes me miss him - even the

musty smell of damp khaki in the rain. We have
been married for five months and have only spent
half a dozen nights together. I managed to get
leave last month and Eddie wangled a sleeping out pass
and we stayed at a B and B in the Dales. Wonderful.

She stopped at a local shop to pick up a sandwich for
lunch and drove to the enormous Montrose Basin behind the
town. She parked so she could look out over the water.
The mud flats were home to thousands of birds, especially
geese whose mournful cries filled the skies at dawn and
dusk. She bit into the sandwich. The bland, slimy ham was
overpowered by too much mustard and the sliced tomato
was hard and unripe. She ate just a little before reaching for
a few more wartime epistles. These were the particular ones
that had concerned and intrigued her and prompted her
quest to Montrose.

14 February 1943

I'm amazed how many good flicks we get at the local
cinema. Dickie took me to see Goodbye Mr Chips on
Saturday and last month it was Jamaica Inn.

Her mother had been married less than a year, yet Eddie
was hardly mentioned, whereas Dickie, whoever he was...
Ann wondered if they had sat in the back row at the cinema.
Was Dickie part of the escapism as well as the films?

167

19 April 1943

I've been rambling a few times at the weekend. The scenery is so beautiful and the wild life is fascinating. Dickie is really knowledgeable about nature. We even saw some deer and red squirrels.

There seemed to be no end to the delights with Dickie. Just how close to nature were those rambles? Unsettled by these disloyal thoughts, she got out to stretch her legs, wondering if Mark was right. A small skein of pink footed geese circled and landed nearby. Most busied themselves feeding but one of them swam over towards her hoping for a few crumbs. She wondered if by some cosmic coincidence this goose was descended from the birds that her mother had watched years ago. Did she feel adrift and separated from her family? Did that make her seek out friendship and maybe more from Dickie?

25 June 1943

Dickie gave me a real treat for my birthday. We cadged a lift to Kirriemuir. It's a quaint market town, the home of J M Barrie who wrote Peter Pan. He had a camera obscura built – talk about magic. You can see the countryside all around and people do not know you are watching them. We watched a couple canoodling in the bushes - quite oblivious!

She had to discover more about her mother and this Dickie character. She looked at the address at the top of the letters where her mother had been billeted and decided this had to be her next destination.

The house was a red sandstone mansion on the outskirts of the town. The paint round the windows was peeling and the curtains were faded but there was a beautiful splash of colour in the garden from some pink rhododendrons. She remembered her mother saying she had once taken a bunch home with her on leave and was devastated when the petals all fell off during the train journey.

She pushed the doorbell, rehearsing her script. It was just as well or she would have been speechless. The man who opened the door resembled her brother so closely. He had the same nose and chin and his ears protruded too. When Mark was young he put sticking plaster on them at night to pull them back. He rejoiced when long hair became fashionable for men. Nowadays with the onset of baldness the ears were over-prominent again. Just like the man in front of her. Fortunately he did not seem to notice her confusion

"I'm really sorry to bother you," she gushed, "but my mother was stationed at the aerodrome during the war and billeted in the town – in this very house. Could I possibly come in and have a look round?"

"Sure. Your mother must have been one of the WAAFs my gran took in. She complained when the War Office cut off the iron railings round the garden to make armaments, but she forgave them when they billeted the girls here. You see she had two sons and always wanted a daughter. She had three girls at a time staying here and she probably spoiled them rotten. Your mother must have been one of them," he repeated, ushering her in to the front room.

"I suppose so. Your grandmother will have missed her sons if they were away in the war and the WAAFs would have been company."

"She had one of her sons here throughout the war - my dad had a reserved occupation as a foreman in a local engineering works. He liked having the girls here too. My mum was one of them – they got married in 1945. He still talks about the war years. I'm John by the way."

"And I'm Ann."

She tried to imagine her mother here. Even now the room had a comfortable, welcoming feel that could have seemed quite seductive to a young woman away from home. Ann smoothed her hair, feeling she was intruding but still curious for more – like hiding behind the settee from monsters on the telly.

"Thanks for letting me see this place. I'm trying to imagine what it must have been like. Do you think your dad would remember any details from back then?"

"Sure to. Do you want to meet him? He lives in sheltered housing as he's frail now but he has all his wits about him. I'm going round this afternoon to give him his bird book."

"Bird book?"

"Yes, he's always had a passion for birds and he loves the Montrose Basin. He's so keen on birds that his nickname is

'Dickie' – Dickie Bird! His magazine from the RSPB is still delivered here and I'm taking it round later. I'll give you his address and you can meet me there about four if you like."

As she walked out into the hallway she noticed a framed photograph of a tall dark haired man holding an enormous ginger cat in his arms.

"That's Dad," John smiled, "and the cat's called Dundee, 'cos they made marmalade there."

He handed her a piece of paper with his father's details which she put in her pocket. Did she really want to meet Dickie who had lived so conveniently close to her mum in this *billet doux*? Mark told her the past should remain history.

She drove down towards the sea and parked, aware that black ominous clouds now sat low over the town. She took a few comfort nibbles of chocolate wondering what to do and read another letter.

3 November 1943

Montrose is like a bubble where everything is fine – we have enough food, unlike poor Mum who is struggling with the rationing. She talks about carrying the ubiquitous gas mask on one shoulder and constant worry on the other. The war seems like a piece of horror fiction. Dickie and I see the Pathé News at the cinema and it seems like the rest of the world is in black and white with only two dimensions. Yet Montrose is in full colour and the people here are real.

171

So was Dickie the real thing?

15 March 1944

It was so lovely to be at home for Xmas and to see you all again and Eddie's leave was a real bonus. I had missed him so much and I was scared I would never see him again.

I really love Scotland with its wild scenery. I even like haggis and whisky (when we can get it) but they put salt on their porridge instead of sugar – it sets my teeth on edge and makes me feel quite queasy.

At last Dickie had vanished and Eddie was back where he belonged. The next letter was not from Montrose – the memories of the posting seemed to have evaporated like Scotch mist.

8 July 1944

I am back at home - discharged because I am expecting a baby. I'm so excited but I worry about how long the war will last. Eddie has been posted overseas – can't say where and I don't know if he even got my last letter telling him he was going to be a dad.

As soon as the MO realised my condition I was packed off with hardly a chance to say goodbye to my mates at the drome or in the town. Of course Mum is delighted but she fusses round me like she's the broody hen. I'm getting so large that Auntie Betty is convinced it's twins!

She took a tissue from her pocket and found the paper with Dickie's details. She glanced at it and dropped it in amazement.

The name of her mother's friend, Dickie, was Iain Carroll; Ann's middle name was Carol and Mark's middle name was Iain. A coded message or simply a secret memento?

She kneaded the wrapper from her chocolate bar into a tight ball and it disintegrated. She shoved it into the ashtray. Her mother had always seemed rather proper and had been horrified when Ann and her friends embraced the freedom of the sixties. What a hypocrite! Or was she just homesick, scared and unlucky?

She picked up the last letter in the pile.

> 10 October 1944
>
> Mum will have told you the news – I have two beautiful babies, one of each. I had the most loving letter from Eddie after the birth. As soon as this awful war is over we will be such a happy family. I can't wait to get a home of our own. I feel our lives have been in limbo for the past few years and now they are just about to begin.

Eddie might not be her real father but she knew he was her real dad. She looked again at the paper with Dickie's address and tore it into tiny pieces. She climbed out of the car, marched over to a nearby bin and threw them away.

As she set off for the south, the setting sun cast a soft pink glow over the landscape. She stopped at a woollen mill for tea and scones and a few gifts. Back in the car, she pulled a luxurious cashmere scarf out of its bag and held its softness against her cheek. She just knew her dad would love it.

THE FUNERAL

Nan Rice

The loneliness. That's what he hated most. The loneliness and the bloody frustration of being locked into his own world. He knew his health was declining - rapidly. His vision had been deteriorating over the last few months, and now he could barely see.

Mostly he couldn't hear either and, on the odd occasion when he thought there was some improvement, he couldn't comprehend the words being directed at him. He knew that, should anyone care to look, they would see the sad remains of a human being. What they didn't know was that he still had the power of thought. Limited, of course, to what he could remember, because he had no way of learning about today's events.

Jake tried to nestle further into his blanket and move his feet on the step of his wheelchair - anything to let himself know he was still of this world. He couldn't dispute the fact that he was well looked after, because there was no shortage of money and his son had chosen the best nursing home in the region, and visited regularly.

And the staff performed their duty well. Each morning a carer would wheel him to the bathroom where two of them carefully stripped, lifted, and lowered him into the bath. He was taken in his chair to the toilet regularly and the soiled nappies were changed. Of course, the nappies were always soiled because he had no bloody control over anything now. Hopefully there was no stench from him. Age was something unavoidable, but to smell like a dirty old person would be horrible.

At meal times spoonfuls of soup or whatever were poured down his throat. There was never a taste of any kind. Never the smell of vegetables or ham or anything used in the making thereof. Yes, it could definitely be said he was in declining health.

As always, his thoughts skimmed back over the years. God, he'd had a great life. Occasionally a little rain had fallen, but he'd taken that in his stride. So much had been packed into his eighty six years. After his poor start to life, success had been his aim in everything he had ever done, and he had travelled the world several times over achieving it.

Now he was tired, and sometimes he could feel the cold nipping his hands and feet, although he knew the nursing home was always warm. Peripheral shutdown, that's probably what it was. He just wished it would go a bit faster so he could meet up with his darling Sarah and his mum and dad.

Now *there w*as a thought. Or several. *His mum and dad.* There was something he could think upon. His mother's funeral. The last connection he had with her.

His recollection of her funeral always began with him

standing at the bar in the private room of the hotel and sipping his whisky while he surveyed the guests. It had been a fair turnout, more people than anticipated. His mother would be pleased if she happened to be looking down on them now. Most of them were family. Some he recognised as acquaintances. Several he had never seen before - probably beneficiaries of his mother's munificence. He was glad to see they were all involved in conversation with someone, and either eating or drinking. Sarah, his wife, was speaking earnestly with his uncle, so he decided to circulate on his own and thank them all for coming.

Before moving off he drained his glass and ordered another whisky. As he watched the level of liquid move slowly towards the optic he recalled the years he had lived with his granny. How poor everyone had been then, although he hadn't realized it. Except for that time he had dived for a football, landed on his knees and torn his first pair of long trousers. His granny cut both legs off at the knees. At school the boys in his class were shouting, "Hay ho Jake-o – are these long shorts, or short longs?" And they had laughed at him. At playtime he had sat alone in the toilet and cried, so deep was his humiliation.

However life then had been a case of make, do and mend and the next day he had got on with his life. They were taught that every penny was a prisoner. Everyone must live within their means. There was no credit system for consumer goods, and the Welfare State cared only for those in deepest poverty, and pride prevented most from admitting to that.

Jake sighed deeply as he thought how times had changed, and brushed a tear from his eye at the loss of these happier days.

"Sir, are you alright?" Jake raised his head to find the barmaid looking enquiringly at him.

"Oh. Oh, yes, thank you. Just a bit upset, y'know. She was my mother."

The girl nodded and discreetly moved away. His mother…there was no doubt in later life that she loved him. But why had she left him on his own so often when he was a young child? And eventually vanished, returning only when he had become a celebrated footballer?

Yes, she had been a complex personality. Today, kind and gentle. Tomorrow, evil, telling lies and causing trouble, setting her relations against each other, at the same time giving the impression of trying to calm the situation. Then there were those she had genuinely helped and showered with gifts and money, asking nothing in return. He had once overheard someone describe her as manic depressive.

He headed to where his three aunts were sitting in a semi circle on high backed wooden chairs. 'Like a witches coven', he thought. Tall women with heavy features and protruberant aggressive chins, they were dressed in black coats, hats and shoes, and clutching black bags on their laps. He was reminded of the hens in his granny's cellar at Alexander Street as each head bobbed up and down whilst making its contribution to the conversation. He thought they looked like they were actually enjoying their elder sister's funeral.

"Sit down, Jake. Take the weight off your legs for a minute. You've been standing a while."

"Thanks, Auntie Nellie." Jake pulled a high backed wooden chair into their conclave and sat down.

"We're just talking about your mother. Katie was bonnie."

"Aye, so she was, Nellie, an' great company. Always game for a laugh and a joke." Jessie, now the eldest, smiled fondly at the recollection.

Jake nodded his agreement. "She was beautiful. I've seen photographs of her when she was young. Tall and thin with big brown eyes and long legs right up to her chin."

Jessie turned towards her sisters. "D'you mind the parties at Edzell in that house Ma took for the holidays during the war? All the yanks that used to come. I don't know how she did it, but Katie always managed to attract plenty of men."

Nellie laughed lightly, then said in a conspiratorial whisper, "It was these lorry drivers that Mrs. Gentles used to take in that started her off," and the three sisters looked knowingly at one another.

Jake asked, "Started her off what?"

Jessie ignored him and went on, "Aye, I remember when we were on our way home from school on a Friday she used to dodge up that close because she knew they'd be up from England. And she was only thirteen. Just a disgrace, she was. My mother would've killed her if she'd known."

"D'you know Jake, your Ma could go onto a bus on her own and come off wi' a man." Agnes tried to assume a look of surprise at how clever her sister had been.

With a curl of the lip Jessie said, "Always thought she was a cut above the rest o' us, so she did, wi' her money and her fancy ways. Insisted she wasn't Dundonian, that she'd been born in Greenock. That the nurses had got her mixed up wi' another bairn in the hospital." Jessie snorted, "She was never in Greenock in her life. Remember the day she got Da the jail? "

"Grandad got the jail. What for?" Jake was aghast.

Jessie pulled a face, trying to convey that the remark had been a slip of the tongue.

"He might as well know now you've said it." Jessie turned to Jake. "Da gave her the last month's rent money for Small's Wynd when we moved to Alexander Street and she went and bought a coat wi' it. Never went near the factor's. He got put in the jail overnight for not paying the rent, and Ma had to scrape, beg and borrow money to get him out."

Jake's stomach churned at the thought. His grandparents had been such decent, hardworking people with eight mouths to feed. "I find that hard to believe. She'd never do such a thing." He couldn't believe anyone could be so heartless. But then, she had left him, hadn't she?

"Aye, but she did. She was furious at not getting her own room in the new house because Ma took in a lodger to help out wi' the money. Katie had to share wi' us three, and our wee brother got yon tiny wee room to himself."

Jake had known the lodger. "I'm sure John wasn't any bother. He was a nice quiet lad. But what about the cellar?

179

Would Granny not have been better making that a place for sleeping instead of keeping chickens?"

Three heads shot round and three pairs of eyes looked disbelievingly at him. It was Agnes who spoke first. "Oh, Jake, no. Ma needed the eggs. What we didn't eat, she bartered with the neighbours or the Scaffy. D' you remember him? Canny Bob? And do you remember the Packyman, Mr. Young? He used to come about tea time on a Friday and talked to Ma for hours. Always full of news, he was. Knew everybody and everything, and he could tell us everything about the Germans and the war and a' that. And mind when Ma got that new linoleum in the kitchen? He said t'her, "I admire yer lay, Missus.""

They all laughed at the absurdity of the statement, although it had been repeated a thousand times, then Nellie, not to be outdone, said, "And do you remember the day he said to us, 'Don't mention Hong Kong because something's happening there.' For weeks we kept reminding each other not to mention Hong Kong. Jeesy peeps, I'd never even heard of Hong Kong."

To Jake's dismay Jessie was determined to return to the subject of his mother's misdemeanours. "Then there was the night Katie was taken to hospital with an abortion. That was the third time she'd messed up. Ma sent me to get you from that house in Carnoustie."

Jake didn't answer, although he did remember the time she was referring to. He remembered as a five year old hiding under the table when she arrived to fetch him. She hadn't noticed the basinful of blood lying beside him. He was appalled that Aunt Jessie seemed determined to carve up his mother's character.

"An d'you remember the time she was supposed to have a bairn adopted? A wee boy, it was." Nellie turned to Jake, "Did you not hear anything about that? He's in America somewhere. A few years back he came over here and met her in the Angus Hotel. She took one of the girls with her, referring to one of Jake's cousins – the younger one, I think. I'm surprised she didn't mention it to you."

Jake was non-plussed. "Another step-brother? You're kidding."

"No. I'm not kidding. She was some girl, your mother." Jessie studied her handbag for a moment, then continued, "Her problem was she hated being poor. Mind you, everybody in Dundee was in the same boat. We a' had to scrape a living. Except for the jute barons that is. They had big houses out the Perth Road in the posh west end, or across the Tay in Newport. The rest o' us had to live wi' the continual loud thudding of the jute mills' shuttles, the awful stench o' the jute, and the constant cloud of dust that hung over Dundee, just to give these rich people the good life. Everybody accepted that was the way it had to be, but Katie envied them."

Nellie nodded in agreement. "She ruined your dad, y' know." He was a fine man. I know for a fact she seduced him on Magdalene Green and got herself pregnant with you just to trap him. Wi' his dad being the west end chemist she thought they were flowing w' money. After they married she ran up big bills in your grandad's name and he couldn't pay them, so she had to take a fur coat, dresses and God knows what all back to the shops."

Jessie decided to take up the story. "Never a week passed but she stayed away one night, or two nights. Your dad wanted to be a chemist like his father, but had to give up his studies to look after you. My mother took you in, and he vamoosed to Nottingham. Mind you, he sent your granny money every week for your keep, and he used to come and stay wi' us sometimes for holidays."

"Yes. I remember the holidays." Jake was torn between wanting to escape from this stream of condemnations and his wish to learn more about his mother.

"And she was a bigamist." Jessie had the bit between her teeth now. "Aye she was. About ten years after she married that foreign Army Major fellow she went down to Nottingham for a few days, with *his* best friend mind you, to discuss divorce with your dad. And not only that, she went to France for two weeks wi' the same man."

Nellie nodded agreement. "Aye. She could be a bad one, our Katie. Ruined a few lives."

Jake couldn't believe his mother and step-father capable of such behaviour. He was relieved to feel the tap on his shoulder.

"I'm just going now, Jake."

"O.K. Aunt Rose, I'll walk you to the door." The old lady took hold of Jake's arm with one hand and leaned heavily on her stick with the other as they made their way slowly to the hotel door where her husband stood waiting. She was in fact a cousin of the three aunts.

"I'm terribly sorry you've lost your mother, Jake. For all she was, she had her good points."

"I don't like the things they're saying about her. It's her funeral for God's sake. They should let her rest in peace."

"Oh, I know. They were always jealous of her looks and personality, and the fact she was never without money and could afford to be well dressed. And Jake, she was a hard worker. She worked in a bakery for a few years when she left school and then got a job in that children's home in Perth and was there until she retired. And you must remember, after your dad, she married a hard working man who made good money, so she was still better off than her sisters and able to live in style. She was a…" Rose hesitated momentarily while she considered how to say it. "She was a prostitute, you know, that was how she always had plenty of money."

"Aunt Rose," Jake was struggling to find words. "That's a terrible thing to say. I don't believe that. Oh, I know she liked men, and was a bit of a good time girl, but please don't say that about her. She wasn't a prostitute, I just don't believe that."

"Oh, Jake." Rose began trembling, upset at Jake's reaction. "I thought I'd better tell you before her sisters told you in a less kindly way. I don't think badly of her for that, Jake, and neither should you. She was driven to it. It was just her way of trying to better herself. God knows, some of the rest of us would have done the same if we'd had the guts." She patted his arm in a consoling gesture as she turned away.

He stood at the hotel doorway, watched Rose and Willie drive off, and allowed himself a few minutes to think of his mother, to remember all the infant schools he had gone to, Ancrum Road, Grove Academy, Victoria Road, all before the age of six, and how he had to sit on the ground outside his house in Ancrum Drive and wait for his dad coming home from work after six. He remembered crying bitterly the day he knew for certain his dad was never coming back. Where had his mother been all these days?

Shrugging off the unhappy, disturbing memories, Jake placed his empty whisky glass on a table, went into the gents', and threw up in the toilet. After the character assassination by the three witches, Aunt Rose's revelation had been like a knife in his heart. He slunged his face with cold water and told himself in the mirror, "No. She definitely was not a prostitute." Once calmed he returned to the lounge and spoke briefly with the departing guests.

"Jake, Jake." He opened his eyes to return to the present. Gentle hands were holding his, and he strained to see who they belonged to. The blur of white told him it was the doctor.

"How're you making out, old pal?" To Jake it was like the voice of an angel. "Are you warm enough?"

Jake tried to shake his head and say, "No."

"What's this on your cheeks? Have you been crying?" He

felt the hint of a caress on his cheek as the doctor wiped his tears away. "I'll ask the nurse to fetch you another blanket," and then he was gone.

Jake wished the kindly man could have stayed a wee while longer. He knew he wouldn't need the extra blanket, but in the brief time he had left he would think of the day his mum and dad had bought him a huge red ball and taken him to the beach at Carnoustie. They'd had a great time. They had all loved each other.

A CHANGE OF ADDRESS

Catherine Young

Agnes stared at the cards.

Miss A. Christie,
formerly of Broughty Ferry,
is now residing at
5, Pitkerro Road, Dundee.

Seeing it in print somehow made it all the more real. It was all over.

"Everything's as you requested?" the stationer asked.

She sighed. So she was *formerly* of Broughty Ferry, *formerly* a highly respected lady's maid. Elegant hotels, ships, the Hill Street house, they were all part of her former self. When she was *Christie*.

"That *is* how you spell Pitkerro Road, isn't it?"

"Pardon?"

"Two r's in Pitkerro, that's right isn't it? Everything's as you wanted?"

No, everything was not as she wanted. Why would it be? To be old, retired, a *former* someone.

"Yes, yes the cards are in order. Thank you. Oh, and some writing paper."

"I'll have to go through the back for the sort you like,

Miss Christie."

Agnes was glad of the reprieve. She sighed and tucked an invisible stray hair into her bun. It was important that shopkeepers knew you nowadays. She'd been with the Misses White through both wars and never gone without: she didn't want to start now, rationing or no rationing. She enjoyed that assistants in Broughty Ferry remembered her preferences.

She supposed she had written rather a lot of letters over the years, especially to her eldest brother and his family in Canada; long newsy letters of her travels and adventures. She hadn't written for a while. But this paper was for a rather difficult letter to her niece in Fife. What to do? What to say? Widowed so young. Maybe extra special writing paper would help.

"Here we are, Basildon Bond."

Deep breath. Head up. Smile. She noticed the assistant had a new haircut that made her look rather like Vera Lynn. Quite becoming, but of course she didn't say. Just a simple 'thank you' then she left.

Purchasing a pottery bed-warmer, or 'pig', was next on her list of things to do. Maybe once she had all her bits and pieces the Pitkerro Road flat would feel more like home and she'd feel more settled.

There was a huge display of pigs outside Spalding's, the chunky utilitarian brown pottery in contrast to a second display of Goss china souvenirs. She picked up a small china plaque with a picture of Broughty Castle. She had a cabin trunk full of travel souvenirs but her mementos were beautiful embroidery from Switzerland, Murano glass from Venice and those fur lined brown elbow-length leather gloves she'd got from the Hudson Bay Trading Company during her last tour of Canada.

It'd been a rather bittersweet tour. A most amazing journey through the Rockies by train, stopping at Chateau Lake Louise. A real once in a lifetime opportunity, she knew. She had sensed the Misses White were aware their 'jaunts' would finally come to an end with the oncoming war and there was a desperation not to miss out on anything.

A lot of her letters to Canada had been planning a visit with the brother she hadn't seen for nearly thirty years during a scheduled two-day stopover in Winnipeg. It ended up a rushed single hour when the Misses White decided to change their travel itinerary at the last minute. Her brother had tutted at her cold hands and taken her to buy the elegant but practical gloves. "A memento of Canada. Think of me every time it's cold in Scotland, Aggie." It'd been years since anyone had called her by her first name, far less Aggie. They scarcely had time to do much else but hug, both knowing they'd never see each other again.

She longed to slip her hands into the gloves; to have her fingers caressed by the soft fur but it wasn't quite fur glove weather yet. Summer was *almost* over and most of the tourists had gone but there were still a few holidaying families and elderly couples wandering around the shops.

"What do you think, Arthur? For our Mary?" An elderly woman in a beige Macintosh held a Goss china plate. "Or those enamel brooches are lovely…"

Instinctively Agnes touched her own brooch. Rose quartz. She'd worn it at her perfectly ironed collar every day for thirty-four years.

"If you won't accept my ring, at least take this. For *friendship*," Alec had said and thrust a velvet box into her hand at the train station. She had looked around guiltily. She was about to go on her first tour abroad with her new employers and she was anxious to impress.

A porter pushed past, toppling a hatbox from a groaning luggage trolley. "Be careful!" she shouted and rushed over, catching Miss White's hatbox but dropping the brooch. She bent down for the velvet box but when she turned Alec was walking away. She never saw him again. She'd heard he'd married and had three children. One child had died of TB and then his son went missing in action in Burma. At least she'd been spared that.

She placed the newly purchased pig at the bottom of her message basket and quickly rearranged her scarf to keep her early morning secret purchase hidden.

The woman who'd been admiring the brooches smiled at her. "Not very elegant, are they? The pigs. But a necessity." Agnes recognised the smug gaze that could see through gloves to ringless third fingers.

"No, they're not, are they?" Agnes rushed out the shop. The souvenirs weren't very elegant either.

She wanted to escape but she'd be in Broughty Ferry for a few more hours yet. She still met Miss McEwan here at

11.15 every Tuesday for a trip to Goodfellow and Stevens - Tuesdays had been their half-day off when they worked. Both women had been on their own one Tuesday the previous summer. A heavy deluge had forced the holidaymakers indoors and both lady's maids had shared a table among the damp throng, tutting at feckless mothers who had forgotten to bring raincoats for children, or umbrellas for themselves. Miss McEwan and Agnes had brought both. A friendship of sorts had been forged.

After their coffee they took a walk along the Esplanade, Miss McEwan taking the lead as always, walking briskly along the pavement that ran atop the wall several feet above the sands. Sitting with their backs to them were three generations of a family in a row of deckchairs. A daughter in shorts and blouse, Mother in a cotton dress and blue cardigan and what she assumed was the Grandmother, like herself in a light coat, but the coat was wide open and she could see Grandmother's shoes were off and her toes wiggled in the sand. Miss McEwan clipped off ahead.

"Hello," the younger daughter in a knitted turquoise bathing suit looked up and saw Agnes smiling. "Do you like my sandcastle?"

"Yes, it's rather splendid with all those shells."

The child nodded. "It's for my dolly. Her old house was bombed." Agnes hovered. All the women looked at each other for a moment.

"I'm sure she'll appreciate your efforts," Agnes said. She could hear Miss McEwan's heels clicking back towards her.

"Come along, we'll be late," she was saying, adding, as soon as they were out of earshot, "You shouldn't encourage her. No one likes a cheeky child."

Agnes looked back at the little family. "Must be about the same age as my poor niece's youngest girl."

Miss McEwan tutted, her hand still on Agnes's arm, steering her away towards the tram stop.

"C'mon, budge up. Let the two old dears sit down."

She winced as the conductress spoke. She'd gone from an 'old maid' to an 'old dear' had she? Miss McEwan appeared not to have noticed and continued with one of her now familiar tirades.

Agnes cut in. "I've been reading about the Bette Davis season at Green's Playhouse. It's been getting awfully good reviews."

"Oh. Really? Anyway, Miss Henderson said…"

"I've decided to go to *Now, Voyager* tonight."

"Pardon? You're going to the cinema? You? In the evening?"

"Yes. Why not? I like Bette Davis."

"But who are you going with?"

She hesitated. "No one."

"You're not thinking of going on your own surely?"

"The world's changed Miss McEwan. I want to go, so I'm going." She chuckled to herself. If Miss McEwan was shocked at her cinema going antics, she'd have apoplexy if she knew about the black market banana hidden in the shopping basket.

The mantle clock in Agnes' front room struck six. She was being ridiculous she knew. This was the third blouse collar she'd ironed (from the point inwards to avoid a crease). People made an effort going out in the evening and for once in her life she wasn't sure what to wear. She didn't want to look too out of place.

She laid the new gloves against the sleeve of her worsted jacket and lifted both to the window light, turning the jacket left and right. French navy indeed. Not a match. She could tell they were just plain old navy when she was in Draffens. What had she been thinking of? She tossed the flat unworn gloves onto the table and the third finger pointed to a cornflower on the cloth that she'd embroidered in the perfect shade, mocking her.

She picked up the gloves, put them back in the Draffens' bag and looked round the room. Where to put them? This was her first home. She'd always been in other women's domains, having to fit in to their ways, and be at their bidding. She couldn't quite decide what to do with the place. Didn't know what *she* liked.

As a lady's maid she'd always had her own *room* though, which didn't always go down too well with the others who had to share – especially when she was younger. *'Thinks she's a cut above, that one'.* She always just rose above it. Best not to get too involved she'd been advised. Advice she'd thought good until now. True, she'd nobody else to worry about. But there was nobody to worry about her either. What if she were to get ill?

So far, the only living souls who had come over the threshold of her flat in Pitkerro Road had been the men employed to carry up her cabin trunk, rocking chair and few other bits she'd accumulated over the years. However, now Miss McEwan had engineered a visit everything would be under scrutiny. She sat in her chair and tried to see the flat through someone else's eyes.

The front room had a high ceiling and pleasant, though rather plain, cornicing and ceiling rose. The windows were large, though not bays. The second room was smaller but adequate really considering the amount of furniture and belongings she had. At least the flat had its own bathroom. She didn't have to endure the humiliation of shared facilities in the close with the neighbours.

Right. What next? The brown pottery pig waited on the table to be filled with hot water to warm her cold bed. She hid it in the cupboard beside the sink. The Basildon Bond notepaper was still on the table, the supportive letter to her widowed niece still unwritten. She suddenly felt guilty. Her niece had no husband so no home or income and two daughters to raise. She had quite a comfortable existence really. But it just wasn't what she'd become accustomed to.

Her beautiful rattan chair had been her pride and joy but somehow lost its allure now the rockers squeaked against brown linoleum. The only thing exciting and exotic was her big black cabin trunk still with the Canada and America travel labels stuck on the sides, left on from the final grand tour with the Misses White. She would put the notepaper and navy gloves away in the trunk for the time being till she found them a home.

Inside the trunk were several wooden cigar boxes and scrapbooks all filled with photos and picture postcards. She couldn't resist having a browse. The Misses White seemed to think she had endless family and friends she sent postcards to. She was a little embarrassed to admit they were for her scrapbooks and didn't like to correct them. Maybe that was why she'd heard nothing from the Misses White since she'd retired? Maybe they just assumed that instead of sending postcards from all her travels, she was now having all those friends and family around for tea.

She found her large green notebook at the bottom of the trunk and traced her finger over the wisteria tendrils painted on the cover. *Becoming an Excellent Lady's Maid.* It had taken her years to write. She'd thought she might become the Mrs. Beeton of domestic service – or at least help her niece's girls to get on but who wanted a lady's maid these days? All the big houses in Broughty Ferry were closing up. She threw the book to the floor. Carefully clipped newspaper articles and advertisements spilled out over the brown linoleum.

Turning defiantly towards the fire she stared at the flames but she couldn't bring herself to throw the book onto the blaze. Retrieving it from the floor, she sat in her rattan chair, rocking it in her arms, gently.

She was getting sidetracked. She still had to get ready for the cinema. Maybe she could send a postal order to her niece? The poor girl had always been a kind obliging sort and Jimmy her father was dead. Her elder brother, Will, would know what to do in this sort of situation but he was in Canada. She was on her own. The last of her generation, and she didn't like it but what could she do?

Collecting the papers from the floor she replaced them in the cabin trunk among all her treasures. But before closing the lid she took her favourite photo from Chateau Lake Louise out of the trunk and placed it on the mantelpiece along with the picture she'd taken of her brother in Winnipeg. She slipped her hands into the fur-lined gloves for a moment, wiggling her fingers in the soft pelt.

The clock struck half past. She couldn't believe the time. She folded the ironing board and stuck a fork into the boiling root vegetables. Still hard. Vegetable stew had seemed a good choice. Put it on at a low heat and let it cook while she was getting ready, but she'd left it all a bit too late. She took a mouthful of half cooked swede and onion, tried to mash up a carrot but it refused to be crushed. She opened the bread bin. Empty. Miss McEwan would be here soon. Nothing else for it, so she placed her napkin on her lap and made the best of it.

She winced and rubbed her chest. Reaching for the Alka Seltzer, her eye landed on the bag with her illicit purchase – a banana. Checking the clock again she ate the banana quickly before burning the yellow skin in the fire. She put on her hat, a last minute check at the mirror – and a snip of a stray whisker – then the doorbell rang.

It was on the way to the Playhouse that she'd first felt uncomfortable and then during the film she was definitely in pain. By the end of the programme she was clutching her chest. Miss McEwan had panicked and wanted to call the doctor. "Don't worry," Agnes said, still gasping for breath. "It's nothing, it's just..." she hesitated, "it's just my angina."

> *Just a note to let you know I've had a change of address. I'm now living with Rina and her girls in Kirkcaldy. The Corporation gave us a lovely three bedroomed house in an awfully good area. We were given priority - because of my heart condition - and Rina's really looking after me.*
>
> *A pharmacist used to live here - Rina knew his housekeeper.*
>
> *Best wishes*
> *Auntie Aggie*

The front gate creaked open and footsteps came up the garden path. She quickly put the rest of the banana into her mouth; another rushed delicacy. It had taken her weeks to track it down but she was getting to know her way around Kirkcaldy now. She folded up the yellow skin, placed it in the fire, covered it with the coals and reaching for her pen and notepaper, pretended to write.

"Hello, it's us," the young girls called.

She swallowed the last of the banana quickly, looked up and winced, a sharp pain in her chest.

Her niece rushed over. "Oh, can I do anything? Should I call the doctor?"

"Oh no, just my angina again," she said and quietly burped.

TWA GULLS AND THREE Js

David Francis

Eh kid mirdir a fush suppir.

- Me an aa. Ehm stehrvin.

Sabbit ehrlay tho.

- Eh, tiz.

Thi Deep Sea'ull no be opin fir awhiyul yit.

- Ehm no gan oot ti sea fir meh suppir.

Naa, yi eejit, naa oot ti sea – thi Deep Sea, thi chippir it thi
fut ih thi Perth Road.

- Iz thit wut itz caad?

Eh.

- Eh nivir kehnt thit.

How no? Itz rittin oan it, plehn ti see – Deep Sea.

- Eh canna read.

How no?

- How no? Coz Ehm a bluddee seagull. Thitz how no.

Si how kin Eh read it then?

- Coz yoora bluddee clivir seagull.

Thitz a shame, izhit? Yirra Dundee seagull in a toon kehnt
fir itz journalism, itz pipirz, Coorier an thi Tuhlay, an yi
canna read. Eh nivir reeullehzd thit.

- Eh kin read thay comics. Thir braa.

Eh, ain o thi grait kweschins ih life, eh, wut ainz thi beh'ir –
Beano ur thi Dandy? Ehm a Beano boy mehsel. Miynd, eh
liyk thit Despriht Dan up in thi Heh Street an heezza Dandy
boy.

- Naa, heezza cowboy.

Eh kehn heezza cowboy. Eh mehnt he wiz in thi Dandy.
Snaffay braa statyoo o um tho. Ji fancy a wee glehde up
thair noo? Thirz iy sum gadgee ur wiyfee feedin thay pijins in
thi City Squerr beh thi Coonsul Buhldin an wi kid gaitcrash
fir a wee snackerull.

- Eh, Eh iywiz enjoy muggin a pijin. Eh hate pijins. Thir
flehin ratz.

Eh hate craaz an aa.

- Howzat?

Weel, jisee this aald boat wir sittin oan? An jisee thit wee
boax oan thi tap ih thit ithir mast owir thair? Kehn wut thiy
creh thit?

- Thi craaz nest.

Eh, igzactly. Weel, izat no daft? Jikehn ehnay seafarin
craaz? Naa, coors no. Shid huv been thi gullz nest. Ehd
huv hud a wurd wi um, thit Captin Scott.

- Mibbee thit wiz eez big discovree – a seafarin craa.

Eh? Eh canna bleev meh eerz. Wut a piyulee hayvirs.
Sumtehms Eh wunner aboot yoo. Birdbrehn. Ahriyt, cumoan,
wi canna leh aboot heer aa diy. Litz hut thi skeh. Wahrull wi
fleh ti? Inti thi toon an gie a pijin a flehg an a black eh? Ur
wi kid follay thi Riversehde Drehv wahr thiv got thit boy

McGonagullz pohtry rittin oan thi street beh thi cundee – thaz thi wurd oan thi payvee, eh? Ur jiwanti tak a wee dehv alang thi ithir wiy – ti thi Ferry? Beh'ir class ih braid alang thair.
- Ir yoo gittin fussy aboot thi class ih yir braid noo? Thaz sumhin fir a boy thit eats as much daid fush as yoo day. Yull be waantin jam oan it nikst.
An thair, meh paal, yi faa oan ain ih thi ithir fiymiss Js o Bonnie Dundee.
- Jumpirz!
Naa! Naebdee nivir sayd nuhin aboot jumpirz! Jam, jam, jam!
- Si Dundeez fiymiss fir three kinds ih jam?
Aa jings! Naa! Jam, jute an journalism. Jino kehn thit? Abdee kehns thit. Abdee firbeh yoo. Miynd Ehm no si shair itz riyt oan thi baa noo.
- How no?
Weel, wahr day yi git jam in Dundee?
- Tescos.
Eh, bit thiy dinna mak it in Dundee tho. Thiy yaizd ti. Thiy yaizd ti mak thit Keillers. Thiy yaizd ti mak thit jute stuff an aa, sacks an tents an stuff, bit noo thiy dinna. Thiv jist got thit Verdant Wurks wahr thiy yaizd ti mak it. Wut an affay reek it hud, eh no? Yi kin smell it yit if yi fleh owir close ti thon plais.
- Eh dun thit thi ithir diy. Thi reek wiz clingin an Eh felt mingin si Eh wehnt up thi Laa fir a blaa. Itz braa, a blaa oan thi Laa. Yi kin see fir miyuls an aa.
Ji liyk thi view?

- Eh hink thir grait, spehshully Kiyull, heez meh faivrit.

Eh mehnt thi view owir thi Tiy.

- Aa! Eh thoht yi mehnt Thi View, kehn thay boyz fay Drehburra. Thir iy singin oan Radio Tiy.

Eh. Yir welcome tay thum, owir loud fir meh taste. Eh prefer thit Michael Marra.

- Welcome – izat no thi nehme ih ain ih thay new buhldinz up beh? Eh mehnt ti ask yi aboot thit coz Eh wiz up thair hayin a raik in a skip roon thi back an a janny cam oot an chased me awa. Naa verra welcome thit, eh no?

Eh hink thitz jist wut thiy creh thi plais. Thiy canna spell tho coz thiy gied it twa Ls. Itz sumhin ti day wi drugs anat.

- Naa? Thitz naa si braa.

Naa, sno bad drugs. Sgaid drugs – fir dohctirs anat - fermircyooticulls.

- Howzat fir dohctirs, then? Shid thiy no be fir fermirs?

Hulp ma boab! It dizna meh'ir.

- An ehdeeaz jist cum inti meh haid.

Thirz a sirprehz. Miynd an no faa aff yir perch.

- If yi tak thi Verdant Wurks an thon Wellcome plais an Thi View, then yi kin siy Dundeez weel kehnt fir three hings.

Eh? Wut?

- Sacks an drugs an rock n' roll.

Oh meh Gohd.

BIOGRAPHICAL AND HISTORICAL NOTES

with accompanying illustrations

'The Prospect of ye Town of Dundee from ye East'

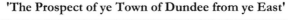

Image from *Theatrum Scotiae* by John Slezer, 1693.

This is the second of Slezer's Dundee prospects and shows the city as it was 73 years after the time in which *The Homecoming* is set. Looking at the town from the east, St Mary's Church tower is clearly visible towards the far end of the town, and the shipping in and around the harbour indicates the busyness of the port. One of the most fascinating details in any of the Slezer views is the group of women in the foreground washing cloth. The custom at the time was for women to 'trample' the washing in large tubs, and you can see three of the figures doing this. Another woman is beating the cloth.

Cathy Whitfield – *The Knowing*

I've been writing short stories, poems and novels for more years than I care to remember, and have had some publishing success along the way. Much of my writing has been inspired by the Scottish countryside, its people and its history, and I'm currently working on a series of novels based on the Tristan and Iseult legend and set in late 5th century Scotland. But on this occasion I decided to focus on an earlier period and to write about the peoples the Romans came across in the late first century AD in the region that would later become Angus. The Romans called them the Venicones, but later this tribe, together with others, would evolve into the confederacy of mysterious peoples known as the Picts, and the land they occupied into the Pictish Kingdom of Circinn.

Christine Mercier – *The Homecoming*

In my work as a freelance translator and interpreter, I have been involved with the Polish community in Dundee. This sparked my interest in the connections between Scotland and Poland not just in the present but in times past. By the second half of the 16ᵗʰ century, when Poland was the grain basket of Europe and Danzig (Gdańsk) was a major port for Baltic trade, there were an estimated 40,000 Scots living in Poland. Many settled permanently, married Polish wives and were granted Polish citizenship. The historic Scottish connection is reflected in names of streets and villages in the vicinity of present day Gdańsk, such as "Skotna Góra" (Scottish Hill), Szotniki and Szoty, while a sprinkling of names such as Ramzy (Ramsey) and Czarmas (Chalmers) in the Gdańsk telephone directory can trace their origins back to Scottish roots.

Migrants to Gdańsk included skilled masons involved in town planning - perhaps they were the antecedants of the Polish builders and plumbers now found on every Scottish building site? So while my character, Jamie Cramer, is purely fictional, he is intended to represent generations of young people throughout the ages who, for one reason or another, decide to leave their familiar home territory to seek fortune and adventure in foreign lands.

Flora Davidson – *Ann Sneeshin's Snuffbox*

I finished a historical novel and looked for another obsession. Living at the mouth of Glen Clova, a place sown with anonymous ruins and no published parish history, I was soon absorbed in finding out. Ruins are yielding to a surveying group from Scotland's Rural Past. Past inhabitants are emerging from the local Kirk Session minutes in a series of vignettes. It was while wading through those for Cortachy and Clova that I came across Sneeshin and Cairnie. The tramps kicked off a series of stories mostly from the same source. Kirk Sessions mostly dealt with the poor and sexually delinquent, and they always seemed to be strapped for cash.

Bob Drysdale – *Admiral Duncan*

I am a retired Building Technology lecturer living at Star of Markinch with my wife and two dogs. I am also a part time book seller and have always enjoyed reading history. The incident I have recounted in my story brings out aspects of the character of Admiral Adam Duncan which are not widely known.

Admiral Adam Duncan (1731 – 1804) was born in Lundie, the son of a Dundee Lord Provost, and joined the navy at the age of 14. While Commander-in-Chief of the British Navy in the North Sea he led his fleet of 24 ships to victory at the Battle of Camperdown in 1797. A grateful nation awarded him titles Baron of Lundie and Viscount Camperdown in addition to the extraordinary sum of £3000 per year as a pension. Part of his family estates now form Camperdown Park in Dundee. Duncan was mentor to another British naval hero, Admiral Lord Nelson, who kept a miniature of Duncan in his cabin while at sea.

A commemorative ceramic bust of Admiral Duncan made soon after the Battle of Camperdown in late 1797 or 1798. The bust is in a local private collection.

Photo courtesy of Clara Young.

Ed Thompson – *The Sporting Life*

After retiring from teaching (Economics), research (Utopian thought) and administration (American Studies) in Dundee University, I worked part-time on the *Dictionary of the Scottish Language*. Here I came across David Haggart, an important source of information on the language of Scottish criminals. At the time of 'The Sporting Life' Haggart was on the run after killing a warder while escaping from jail. Captured in Ireland a year later, he was tried at the High Court in Edinburgh and hanged on 18 July 1821. He had just turned 20. While in the condemned cell he dictated an account of his life: he was proud of his skill as a pickpocket, but had no objection to mugging, burglary, card-sharping, smash-and-grab and shoplifting. He showed little remorse for his crimes, which he referred to as 'sport'.

Ann Prescott – *Gleaners of Nature*

I began writing fiction when I retired from a lifetime working with facts as a chemist. I find it's a hard habit to kick however so whereas Eliza's background is pure fiction, William Gardiner's life (1809-1852) is reasonably well documented. Botanist, umbrella-maker and poet, he published the first detailed account of the Flora of Angus (then called Forfarshire) in 1848. He married Elizabeth Smith in 1843/4 and she pre-deceased him by two years leaving their five-year old son. William Gardiner's poem "The Laced-winged Fly" is quoted in William Norrie's *Dundee Celebrities of the Nineteenth Century*, published in 1873. William Gardiner's Diary for 1827, his letters to his wife, obituary notices and papers relating to 'Gleaners of Nature' and the 'Rational Institute' can all be found in the Lamb Collection in Dundee City Library.

Gill Blackmore – *Dead Ed*

As a dog owner I have often walked along East Haven beach and would stop to read the memorial plaque beside the car park which gives a potted history of the 'Ha'en', as it was known. I thought how sad it was that such an obviously bustling little village which boasted 34 households, an inn, a baker's, a grocer's, fishermen, weavers, railway workers and farm workers, had been so devastated by not one but two terrible epidemics, only a year apart. In 1848 Scarlet Fever killed a sixth of the population, mainly children, and in 1849, an outbreak of Cholera was equally fatal.

As I walked my dogs, I would often wonder just what it would have been like during this time of death and disease and how many families may have been wiped out and who had been lucky enough to survive. As I walked, and with the Roots project in mind, Jason's voice popped into my head and I told his story.

I would like to thank Carnoustie Library for their help with my research and I dedicate this story to our recently lost but always remembered puppy, Mini.

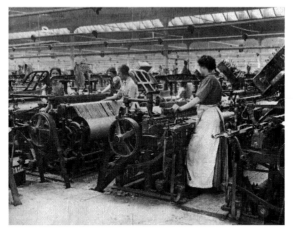

Dundee mill workers c.1908.
Photo courtesy of Dundee University Archives.

Farm life in the late 19th century as seen at Craigie Farm, Dundee.
Photo courtesy of www.photopolis.org.uk/

Beth Blackmore - *Small Sacrifices*

I was born in Glasgow in 1940 but now live in Carnoustie. Until I retired I was head teacher of a multi-lingual primary school in the west end of Dundee. My main interests are reading and writing, and cycling with my husband on our tandem.

The shawl-clad lassies who worked in the Dundee Jute Mills during the mid to late 19 Century were a unique breed of independent, stubborn and vociferous young women who evolved from the intolerable poverty of life at home and the cruel hardships of work in the mills to gain a small degree of organised power. Their sacrifices and sufferings, and their endless struggles to improve things are embodied in the character of Mary Gartshore in *Small Sacrifices*.

Jean Langlands- *Mrs Dargie's Revenge*

When I was young I had the desire to be a writer but the advice I was given was to find myself a proper job. And so I trained as a nurse and forgot all about writing, until recently, when I retired. I wanted to write a story set in rural Angus and by chance came across the story of a local girl who worked on an Angus farm. Her liaison with the farmer's son caused her to meet with an unfortunate end. She was poisoned with arsenic and the farmer's wife came under suspicion. In this fictionalized version I have changed some of the details of the story and given it a surprise ending.

David Carson – *The Coffin Road*

I spent almost all of my working life in the teaching profession, firstly in Glasgow and latterly in Perth and Angus. Now that I have retired, I'm able to pursue my other interests - cycling, squash and in particular hillwalking - to a greater extent. I'm married with three grown-up daughters.

There are few indications of coffin roads on maps; references survive in the names of physical features, like the lugubriously named Lochan nan Corp in the Trossachs. It was while reading about hillwalking routes in the Angus glens that I came across accounts of coffins being carried over the hills from Braemar into Glen Isla and Glen Prosen. Through further research there emerged stark but fascinating descriptions of the hardships and solemnity associated with carrying a coffin good distances over hilly ground. Imagination then invented the circumstances surrounding such an event. My thanks to those who helped so willingly and constructively in the writing of the story.

Lesley Holmes – *The Ballad O' The Chieftain*

I first became interested in creative writing two years ago and have found it a welcome change from my work as a process specialist. Although born in Yorkshire, I have lived and worked in Dundee for many years. My keen interest in poetry inspired this ballad which captures the story of the strong-hearted, resourceful men of Dundee who endured icy seas, howling winds and freezing fogs to earn their pay – in particular the crew of *The Chieftain*. A Dundee whaler in its first year in the fleet, *The Chieftain* sailed to the polar ice fields in 1884 with its crew of mainly Dundee men. The story tells of the dangers they faced and what happened to the boat crews under the command of Captain John Gellatly, who was making his maiden voyage.

The *Balaena* was one of the most famous whalers to be based in Dundee and sailed its last voyage in 1892 under Captain Alexander Fairweather. The trip to the Antarctic yielded two whales and 2500 seals, which produced half a ton of whalebone and 50 tons of oil. Whalebone was used, among other things, for making ladies' corsets, while the oil was burned in lamps, etc.

Photo courtesy of www.photopolis.org.uk

The impressive corner building at the south end of Dundee's Commercial Street at its junction with Dock Street housed the offices of various shipbrokers and engineers. The Dundee Gem Line Steam Ship Co. Ltd, featured in *Blackheart*, was also based in the building.

Photo courtesy of www.photopolis.org.uk

Amanda Barclay – *Blackheart*

As a fifth generation Scottish engineer, I find writing a welcome change from the more practical aspects of my work. I live and work in Dundee and enjoyed researching the maritime history of the city. The fleet of steamships owned by Gem Shipping Line of Dundee was busy on the flax run between the Baltic ports and Dundee though they also found plenty of cargoes from Spain, Greece and the Middle East. The fleet of the *Amethyst, Beryl, Diamond, Garnet, Jasper, Opal, Ruby* and *Sapphire* were all - with the exception of the *Sapphire* - built in Dundee at either Gourlays or W B Thompson's yard.

Roddie McKenzie – *The Old Man and The C*

I have worked in many occupations, including twenty-five years as a biochemical researcher. I also lived in Canada for ten years and often use my own life experiences as a background for my work. On this occasion, however, I have tried to retell, from a novel angle, Toshie McIntosh`s story and to highlight the number of whaling crew who got a start as stowaways as an escape from dismal mill conditions and poverty. Toshie was right, the trade was essentially finished by the 1890s - after a tremendous loss of ships and endured misery for their crews. The *Polar Star* that the lads were trying to stowaway on was lost on the voyage to Hudson Bay. The enigma of what happened during Toshie`s 'lost voyage' is maintained. Norman Watson`s, *The Dundee Whalers*, was invaluable for research.

Faye Stevenson – *Two For The Price Of One*

Photo courtesy of Dundee University Archives

Mary Lily Walker

In between teaching and helping my husband run our N.E. Fife Hotel, I try to find time to write. As part of my research for this story I visited Grey Lodge Settlement where the work ongoing today is as impressive as it was when the Settlement was first set up by Mary Lily Walker (1863 – 1913). As a young woman, she became conscious of the appalling living conditions of the poor. She wrote detailed official reports on health and housing and founded Grey Lodge Settlement in 1888 as part of the University Settlement movement. She transformed Dundee with baby clinics, health visitors, school dinners, children's convalescent holidays, and clubs for all (including after-school) groups - all this in less than 15 years

John Mooney – *Mallet*

As a golfer myself, I was drawn to putting the game at the heart of my story. Early shafts for golf clubs were usually made from whatever local wood was available but when the game spread to America in the early 1800s hickory began to be used due to its availability and suitable properties. Hickory was very durable and became the standard until steel shafts were introduced in 1925.

The introduction of steel shafts met with some resistance particularly from the more traditional player who considered their introduction as making the game too easy since with matched sets of steel shafted clubs only one consistent swing was required regardless of which club was being played whereas each hickory shafted club required its own individual action. By 1926 the United States Golf Association accepted the use of steel shafts and in 1929 the R&A followed suit.

1958 view from the former Bruce Hotel, Carnoustie, over Hotel tennis courts and Dalhousie Golf Club towards old starter's box and pavilion and the 18th green of the championship course.

Photo courtesy of DC Thomson & Co.

Jane O'Neill – *Ba, Ba, Da, Da*

Several of my short stories have been inspired by childhood and family memories of Dundee and it is no surprise therefore that *Ba Ba! Da Da*! is set in the area of the 'Burn', near The Westport, where a generation of my family lived and worked. You will not find the Scourinburn – as it was previously known – on a modern map of Dundee, or indeed any of the tenements that housed the factory workers, but the old St Mary Magdalene's Church still stands in Blinshall Street. Maggie, a character in *Ba Ba! Da Da*! caused a stooshie by getting married in this church!

215

Gaye Manwaring – *Between The Lines*

I am a senior lecturer in education at the University of Dundee, teaching mid-career professionals. I have lived in Scotland for over forty years though I was born in England. My parents, Joan and Len Manwaring, were both in the RAF in the Second World War. I am grateful for their memories and anecdotes which inspired the background details for this piece of fiction. My mother was a wireless operator in the south of England. My father was stationed at Montrose Aerodrome while he trained as an instructor pilot. Montrose was the first operational air station in Britain in 1913. It closed in 1950 and it is now a heritage centre. There is more information on the following website:

http://www.rafmontrose.org.uk/

Hawker Furies of No. 8 Flying Training School, RAF Montrose flying over the town C1938. These were fighter trainers used by the pupils in the final stages of their training and remained in service until 1940.
Photo courtesy of Montrose Air Station Heritage Trust

Nan Rice – *The Funeral*

My working life has been varied, interesting and, at times, highly amusing. Leisure activities have included drama and stand up comedy. Short story writing is my latest venture. My character, Katie, is based on a real person. The lady was in her early sixties when I met her, beautiful, well groomed, poised, wealthy, and with an expansive personality. In time I learned she had always pursued her own selfish ends, ignoring the hurt and misery she caused to others. An interesting and complex person, her life had been one long ego trip, wracked on occasions by her own devils. It must be said, however, in support of her chosen way of life, she had risen above her beginnings, and achieved her aim.

Poverty, deprivation, and war had combined to form Katie's character, and one must acknowledge that like her, there must have been many others driven to extreme behaviour.

Catherine Young – *A Change of Address*

I had mostly features published in the 80s and early 90s and am now enjoying a return to writing – this time fiction. My stories have appeared in local anthologies and been selected for performance at *Winter Words*, 2007. As a child I was fascinated by my granny's stories. Auntie Aggie is one of several incredibly strong, independent women in our family tree. This is the first time I've used one of them as inspiration

217

for my writing.

Aggie – supposedly at death's door – *did* go to live with her niece (my granny), enabling them to get a good house. However her angina turned out to be indigestion and she continued to live there for more than 20 years. The two women pooled resources ensuring both of the girls got a good education and career. Neither of them went into service. Although Aggie refused to share her black market banana, she did gift her cabin trunk to one of 'Rina's girls' when she too emigrated to Canada as a newly wed. I now have the gloves and they're still fabulous.

(Thanks to Margaret for her childhood memories.)

Broughty Ferry is the opening location for *A Change of Address*. This photo shows a parade at Broughty Esplanade. Date unknown.
Photo courtesy of D.C Thomson

David Francis – *Twa Gulls and Three Js*

I have always been an avid reader and am now pursuing a long held ambition to learn more about the craft of writing. This piece started as an exercise in dialogue and dialect, trying to make the most of the 'aa' and 'eh' sounds after I'd read somewhere the somewhat unkind suggestion that broad Dundonian bears a resemblance to the sound of seagulls. The dialect itself can be regarded as uniquely rooted in Dundee and I hope I've managed to do it justice. I've also tried to include as many references as possible to Dundee icons and landmarks.

UDEMSA

University of Dundee Extra-Mural Students Association

represents students taking courses provided by the Department of Continuing Education, University of Dundee. These include classes held in Dundee, Perth and Forfar on . . .

Art History, Media, Music; Behavioural Studies and Personal Development; Computing; Creative Writing; Fine Art and Design; History and Archaeology; Literature; Management and Professional Development; Philosophy and Religion; Science and Nature; Social Studies.

Course Contact: Jill McKay, Continuing Education, University of Dundee

UDEMSA Contact: Dr Edward H. Thompson, *email:* EHThompson@Dundee.ac.uk